Henry

From as high up as he was, Henry had a clear view of the entire landscape below him; rolling hills and fifty shades of green. The infamous carrier pigeon soared and swooped through the clear blue sky, on his way back to Hillside Farm, in the process of completing another one of his important messages. This particular message was one of such importance that Henry had been given full airspace clearance by the Carrier Pigeon Air Control Unit and he was operating on a minimum tolerance basis, meaning that he had authorisation to fly without speed restrictions and that the Eagle Air Patrol would turn a blind eagle-eye to any dangerous manoeuvres Henry might perform mid-flight. He regularly reached speeds of up to 100mph as he winged through the cool air, his smooth and well-groomed feathers hardly being ruffled by the noisy wind. So experienced was Henry, and so well trained was he, that he had become one of the few homing pigeons in the whole countryside to be able to deliver messages in both directions. Of all the other pigeons he knew (and him being such a famous pigeon, he knew many thousands of other well trained carrier pigeons), only a very small percentage of them were able to operate in this way. It enabled Henry to deliver messages or small packages between his clients, to and from desired destinations, rather than simply from one location back to his base in Hillside Farm. Of course, this brought about many admirers and countless requests for specific tasks, such as the one he was completing today.

Hillside Farm had become a notorious tourist spot for many animals during the recent months, following rumours of a tale about how a large Wolf had been overpowered by a seemingly even larger pig. Creatures of all shapes and sizes, of all species and classes, would visit the farm to hear of the exciting and, in some cases, terrifying story. The heroes of the saga, three little pigs and their father, Jeremy, would retell the events of the adventure, as listeners sat around dimly lit fires, engrossed in the words and whispers of the now cult-status pigs. The three brothers, Stanley, Harvey and Davey, would take turns to re-enact the main highlights of the quest and Jeremy would add in little bits of background information as they went, making sure the avid spectators didn't miss out on anything important. Stanley would demonstrate his prowess with a staff and retell of his heroics when saving one of his brothers from certain death, after a fall on one of the perilous cliffs of Springfield Mount. Davey would excite his audience with a detailed rendition of how the trio worked together to overcome a vicious family of hungry and dangerous foxes. The visitors, who always provided generous gifts for the experience, would be enthralled by Davey's theatrical accounts of how he cleverly used a little mirror to blind the largest of the foxes, just at the right moment, allowing his brothers to carry out their ambush. Harvey, who was happy for his brothers to take most of the acclaim for the storytelling, provided a lavish full-course taster menu for the guests, delighting them with his well-known classics of stuffed peppers or vine leaves. And he always had something new on the little specials blackboard for the hors d'oeuvre or dessert courses. Often, guests were left speechless at the aromas and taste sensations that would delight their palates, and they could be frequently seen pausing for a moment after a mouthful, allowing for the time necessary to appreciate the multitudes of flavours.

Hillside Farm had indeed become a hub of activity since the Wolf was last seen tumbling down the cliff side of Wakeman's Hill into the raging Silkstream River below. And life on the farm was good. The healthy and happy pigs generated an excellent manure for the soils. Farmer George's crops were improving with every cycle of the seasons and the other animals on the farmstead lived contently in the blissful surroundings. All except Billy the Goat and Johnny the Cock. They no longer lived on Hillside Farm. As a result of the improved crops, both in quantity and quality, Mary and George had decided to expand their business a little. Being quite the entrepreneur, Mary came up with the proposal one evening over dinner with her husband, explaining to him the benefits of venturing out and setting out the details of the expansion. Not a large scale development, just something that would work alongside what they were already doing and provide an extra income for a rainy day. Mary enthused about the location she had discovered; an idyllic plot of farmland and a large island, separated by a crooked strait of water and connected by a rickety old bridge. So enticed by her description of the scene was George, he had to go and see it. He too fell in love with the plot the moment he set eyes upon it and the two of them completed the purchase later that day, before arranging for Billy the Goat to be reunited with his parents. Billy's parents had been loaned to Buck Lane Grange, a newly started neighbouring farm, to help settle in some new animals and get some revenue going with dairy produce. Johnny the Cock was also to be sent along with Billy in order to roost with a new batch of hens, which Mary had acquired from another nearby farm. The lushness of the meadow was so intense that Mary was confident that Billy and his parents would flourish there, maintaining the grass and providing milk of the highest quality.

Billy and Johnny had been inseparable since birth and were brought up by Billy's parents before the four of them became separated. Despite the fact that Billy and Johnny were upset to be leaving the familiarities and luxuries of Hillside Farm, they were glad that they were both being moved together, and overjoyed that they would be brought back together with Billy's parents, whom Johnny pretty much considered to be his own parents too, such was the devotion they had shown to him in the past. Upon arriving at their new home, Billy and Johnny immediately set about exploring the meadow and getting acquainted with the new hens and the other wildlife. The short time they had spent at the meadow had been a very positive experience; Billy's coat had never looked so healthy, his mother's milk was, as Mary had predicted, of an excellent standard, and Johnny's hens were producing eggs at a very productive rate. It was only a short drive away from Hillside Farm and already, George and Mary were reaping the benefits of their new business venture.

So as Henry continued to hurtle through the sky with the wind whistling in his auriculars, Harvey drummed his trotters impatiently, as he sat in his mud pit, waiting for a response to the mission he'd given to Henry a short while earlier. Edward, the second in command of the Eagle Patrol Unit, soared high above Henry and looked down upon him with contempt. He didn't understand why a mere pigeon would be given such freedom to fly in any way he wanted and why the Air Control Unit would have requested free airspace in which for him to travel. Edward the Eagle swooped down and cruised above Henry, his enormous wings shadowing the little pigeon. Henry looked up and snarled at Edward. There had always been a great deal of animosity between the two groups of birds. It was the job of the carrier pigeons to deliver messages, sometimes urgently, through the skies and on the other hand, it was the responsibility of the eagles to patrol the environment, ensuring the safety of the other birds and that all flight animals were in a suitable condition to fly. On many instances in the past, some pigeons had been held up by the Eagle Patrol Unit (in their opinions, unnecessarily) and lost business or had their reputations destroyed as a result. Henry recalled one date specifically when Edward himself had stopped Henry to check his feathers and enquire about his business. Henry had been as accommodating as possible, yet he believed that Edward was purposefully taking his time and being unreasonably thorough with his questions and checks. On that day, due to how late Edward had made him, Henry had come close to losing a particularly important client and Henry vowed never to trust the rigorous eagle again. Their eyes met and Edward snarled back at the grey dove and gave out an echoing squawk which deafened Henry momentarily. Knowing that there wasn't a great deal Edward could do this time; Henry saw his chance for some retribution. He artfully dodged to the left and quickly swished to the right before performing a deft somersault, enabling him to change direction in the blink of an eye. Henry came out of the somersault and as gracefully as a ballerina performing a well-practised pirouette, ended up directly above and behind the miserable old patrol bird. And it just so happened that at that very moment, Edward did indeed blink. Right before his very eyes, it seemed as though that pesky pigeon had completely vanished. With his squawk still reverberating around the clear skies, Edward looked around in all directions, desperate in the hope that he wasn't about to be undone by a pitiful pigeon.

But he had been undone. Well and truly. After all, Henry was no ordinary pigeon. He was a highly skilled flight master; a thoroughbred of the skies, from a long line of accomplished and gifted ancestors. He was born to do this, literally. Henry's great, great grandfather was the heroic First World War messenger pigeon, Cher Ami, famous for his valiant deeds of delivering messages above enemy lines in the throes of war. Despite being shot and critically injured during his final mission, Cher Ami continued to brave the skies and deliver his message home. Among other injuries, the leg to which his note was attached was badly damaged but his mission was a success and he was awarded the French 'Croix de Guerre' medal, noting his heroic service. President Wilson, a distant relative of Henry's, was another wartime pigeon who suffered and survived terrible injuries at the hands of German gunfire. His record-breaking flights were referred to countless times during Henry's training and he was one of Henry's inspirations throughout his days as a squab. Like many of Henry's ancestors, President Wilson was taxidermied and upon completion of his first stage of training, Henry was rewarded with a visit to a window ledge of one of the many windows looking into the Pentagon in America. From this viewpoint, Henry had an excellent opportunity to examine his idol in detail and it remains one of Henry's proudest moments. It didn't stop there; Henry's grandfather, named G.I. Joe, continued the tradition in fine style during the Second World War when he delivered crucial communications between British troops in an Italian town and the allied Headquarters. Legend states that G.I. Joe was responsible for saving thousands of lives when he flew twenty miles in approximately twenty minutes to deliver a message of the allied troops' position, preventing them from being bombed by their very own forces. G.I. Joe was awarded the 'Dickin' medal for his feats of bravery.

In the determined mood Henry was in, Edward didn't stand a chance. His huge, powerful wings beat against the wind like a giant rug on a clothes line. Against a larger, less agile bird, he would have had no problem in slowing down and arcing through the air to gain an advantage. But the cunning messenger was always one step ahead, watching Edward from above and second guessing his every move. Edward feinted to the left and swooped down, preparing for a loop-the-loop type manoeuvre. In response, Henry opened his wings and came to an almost immediate halt in mid-air, before darting southwards in a falcon-style nose dive. He rocketed towards the Earth and, without slowing, entered the thick treetops of the forest below, tilting and flipping like an x-wing fighter. By the time Edward had completed his corkscrew (during which he'd achieved absolute ceiling, meaning he had reached the maximum height that he could maintain under standard air conditions), he felt light-headed and disorientated. The old bird was getting on a little and wasn't used to performing such tricks; not at that speed or height and certainly not under the stressful circumstances of being humiliated by a lowly pigeon. He quickly reduced his altitude and in a last ditch effort to make amends, he searched the skies once more, furiously twisting his neck in all directions. Unbeknown to him, in all the furore of the chase or the search, Edward found himself far too close to the very treetops into which Henry had disappeared. He clattered into the highest branches of the tallest tree in the forest and somersaulted inelegantly through the boughs, in a most undignified manner. The commotion his crash landing made had alerted the attention of two inquisitive squirrels, who scampered along the branches and stood on their hind legs, staring with delight at the sight before them. They began to squeak. Quietly and intermittently at first, but their laughter (and Edward just knew they were laughing) grew louder and louder, until they were rolling on their backs and tummies; Edward was sure they were banging their little fists into the wooden branch upon which they lay, as if it was the funniest thing either of them had ever seen. And it probably was.

Gliding just feet from the forest floor, Henry was unaware of the unfortunate tumble that Edward had suffered, so he cautiously lifted himself up through the leaves and out into the open once more. A quick scan informed him that the skies were clear and, wondering what had become of his pursuer, Henry continued on his way to finally deliver his message to Harvey. As he flew down and landed on the fencepost that enclosed the pigsty in Hillside Farm, Henry spotted Harvey wallowing in the mud, a content yet disgruntled look on his chops. He wasn't used to be made to wait by Henry and he had a busy schedule to stick to, not that it showed as he slopped a generous dollop of sticky sludge onto his belly and rubbed it into his skin.

"It's about time Henry." Harvey said. "I've got lots to prepare for and you've been keeping me waiting. Timing is everything."

"Yes, sorry Harvey," replied the messenger. "I had a run in with Edward the Eagle and I had to shake him off my tail. Even though I had special clearance for the mission, he was still on the lookout. It was almost as if he was just flying around, waiting for me to turn up. Hasn't he got anything better to do?"

"Yes, yes. Well you're here now, that's all that matters," said Harvey, slowly standing up out of the slurp and splattering his way over to where Henry sat. "Do you have it?" he asked, excitedly.

The Crooked Strait

"Look at this place," Gruff said, proudly. "What a beautiful meadow. I've never tasted such grass." He looked lovingly at his son, Billy, who was prancing around the field and chewing hungrily at a mouthful of thick, green sward. Gruff and his partner, Sally, were overjoyed to have been reunited with their son and, of course, with Johnny the Cock. It had been many months since they had last seen each other and even though the couple had enjoyed their time at their previous farm, they had always longed to be returned to their lad and his soulmate. Farmer George was a kind-hearted man and from the minute he had shipped them across to the other farm (which had been recently established) to help some of the more nervous animals settle in to their new environment, Gruff was confident that he wouldn't be away from his family for too long. And sure enough, here they were, cavorting amongst the grasses as if they'd been here forever. Despite the fact they'd only been living in their new home for a few days, it felt like they belonged here.

Their new surroundings were undeniably idyllic. They had a great, beautiful meadow all to themselves, along with a large goat pen for Gruff and Sally, and a separate kidding pen for Billy and Johnny. So independent had they become, that Mary thought it would not be appropriate for all of them to live together under the same roof. The kidding pen was connected to the main shelter via a simply constructed passageway and the animals came and went as they pleased. George and Mary had made sure that all their creature comforts had been considered. The field itself was well cordoned off with a strong, wooden-poled fence, preventing the goats from straying onto the nearby road. Walkers were still able to interact over and through the barrier and the new residents were already becoming popular with a few small groups of children who walked past the field to and from school each day. Their shelter sat upon the mound of the meadow, looking down on the pastures below. In one section, there was a sturdy chicken coup, complete with comfortable nest boxes for egg-laying and perches for the hens to sleep. The hens had ample quarters in which to exercise and they were protected by an overhead mesh, to thwart any hungry foxes or large birds, intent on snatching one away for dinner. Johnny entered the coup through a clever little cat-flap style device which Farmer George had inserted into the side of the shack; a small fob attached to Johnny's collar allowing him access when he pleased.

Two thirds of the field was surrounded by the aforementioned fencing. A meandering strait of water ran alongside the final third of the meadow, separating it from an adjacent island, in which a large bull resided. Billy and Gruff would walk along the stream each morning, playing with their reflections in the ripples and Gruff would teach Billy about the different kinds of stream life whenever they saw something new. On this particular morning, while Sally was grazing up on the mound, Gruff, Billy and Johnny were strolling along the brook as usual when a loud bellow rumbled across the landscape from the island. Billy and Johnny cowered in fear as the deep, thunderous cry rolled around the hills.

"That, my dear boys, was the bull who lives on the island," said Gruff, looking down seriously at the two frightened souls. The final aftereffects of the yell were just fading as Gruff continued. "You're not ever to go into that field, do you hear me?"

"Yes Dad," said Billy.

"Johnny? You as well."

"Yes Dad," replied the rooster, looking down at his feet, sheepishly.

"If the rumours about that bull are true," Gruff went on, "he's a dangerous and aggressive individual and your mother and I will be very angry if we find out that you've gone over there, do you understand?" It was uncharacteristic of Gruff to be so assertive and direct with the two youngsters. They were far more accustomed his gentle and playful side so when he spoke to them in this way, it really hit home. He continued to explain that during the time he and Sally were away, they had heard lots of frightening stories about that island. It was the one thing that had niggled in the backs of their minds prior to the move, but when they had heard George and Sally discussing the bridge one evening, they were satisfied that their meadow was perfectly safe.

Although one side of the landmass was accessible from the bridge, the rest of the perimeter was surrounded by a treacherous and rocky shoreline that made it almost impossible to travel to by boat. The wooden platform connecting the meadow to the prohibited island was a ramshackle of a bridge. It creaked in the slightest of winds and seemed to be waiting to collapse into the waters below at any moment. It had, however, been standing for many years in that condition and local legend told of stories about a strange creature that used to live beneath it. It was from this tale that the bridge got its name, The Troll's Arc. Many hundreds of years ago, it was fabled that this hobgoblin-type creature would hide underneath the bridge and jump out at anyone trying to cross it. The island to which the bridge provided access was rumoured to contain a rare herb that travellers from around the world would come to collect. The plant, known as Clary Sage, was known for its medicinal and culinary properties and was considered to be a collector's item. Every now and then, in search of this unusual plant, a new explorer would attempt to use the bridge, in the hope that they might receive a handsome sum of money for just a small handful. Journeymen would return home, usually empty handed and laden with excuses to explain their failure. Stories of a giant ogre, or a murderous monster, would generate huge interest in this inconspicuous location, and perhaps some adventurers would make it onto the island and return home, weighed down with their trophy flower. However, the mysterious 'creature beneath the bridge' story faded away, as more flavoursome herbs became popular, and the bridge was left to groan with the burden of its own weight and warp with the cycle of the seasons.

And this was the reason why Gruff knew he and his family would be totally safe in their new home. A bull with such a reputation and with a bellow like the one still ringing in poor Billy's ears would certainly be too heavy to walk across The Troll's Arc. Surely, one careful hoof, placed gently down onto the first crumbling slat as a tester of sturdiness, would bring the structure crashing down into the stream. For many years, the bull had lived on the island, feeding off the tall grass, seemingly content in his solitude. Not that he had any choice in the matter, but Gruff had weighed up the options and allowed himself and his family to be relocated to their new abode. At least that's what he told his family; not only to put them at ease but to also save a little face. George and Mary had put him there and that was where he was going to stay. As always, he trusted in his owners and genuinely believed that this new location was the start of fresh and exciting adventures. After all, what could a buck such as Gruff enjoy more than spending each day in a charming, lush meadow, surrounded by his family and nature's tranquil beauties?

Happy in the knowledge that the bellowing bull would not be able to leave the island via the bridge, Billy and Johnny continued to enjoy themselves, playing by the riverside and on the bales of hay dotted around the meadow. Mornings and afternoons, they would entertain the school children through the fence, bleating and cock-a-doodle-dooing at them as they strolled past. In the evenings, the four of them would talk about the months during which they were separated. Billy and Johnny always loved to hear about how Sally nurtured many of the young animals that she roomed with by pretending to be their nanny. She would tell of feeding time; how she had to make sure the infants ate the right amounts and at the correct times. She'd talk about calming some of them down during restless nights, or returning the odd sleep walker back to its bed. Gruff spoke enthusiastically of how he would organise group games in the field, encouraging the animals to play nicely together and helping them to learn the importance of getting along with all creatures, not just those of the same species. Billy and Johnny would recall their own experiences of Hillside Farm and their parents would listen keenly to stories about Claire the horse and Cynthia the sow, two of Sally's close friends before she was moved. They did, however, listen with increasingly concerned expressions when Johnny told of the parties that began to happen at Cynthia's. One evening, forgetting that he was talking to

16

his surrogate parents, Johnny let slip that he and Billy had tried a chamomile concoction that had a particularly soothing effect, especially on small animals. Despite what they had been taught at farm school, the two of them had ignored the warnings and experimented with this relaxing tea combination on more than one occasion. It was safe to say that Sally was far from impressed and she kept a close eye on the little tearaways over the course of the following days, making sure that they were both behaving appropriately. It was also safe to say that Billy and Johnny had a man to man chat about knowing what to say, when to say it and who to say it to.

As the sun rose one morning, spreading light and warmth across the picturesque meadow, Gruff was standing at the foot of the bridge, looking across the stream towards the island. Billy and Johnny were running circles around each other, dodging in and out of the hay bales, when Billy saw his father and stopped. He motioned to Johnny with a cock of his head in Gruff's direction and they strutted down to the river to join him.

"Do you know what this stream is called, Billy?" he asked as they approached.

"Yes Dad," the kid replied. "It's called Silkstream. I know that because when the pigs returned from their adventure, they told us little bits of what happened. When Jeremy fought the Wolf, he ended up disappearing down the cliffs of Wakeman's Hill and into the Silkstream River."

"That's correct," said Gruff. "The river's source is high

up on Springfield Mount and it meanders down through Seeker's Peeks and Wakeman's Hill, until it travels under our little bridge here and out into the sea." Billy and Johnny loved listening to Gruff teach them about the environment; he always had an interesting snippet of information or a quirky fact about the area. "Do you know where the river got its name from?" he continued, knowing full well that they didn't. Not waiting for a response, he carried on. "You already know a little bit about the history of the bridge and creature that used to live beneath it. Well during that time, this stream was lined with mulberry bushes, which is what silkworms live on. This river was the only other place in the world other than China where silkworms could survive. They must have been brought here by a merchant or traveller of some kind when they were looking for the Clary Sage. So for many years, the stream was ravaged by traders looking for the silkworms. Eventually, the numbers declined and traders stopped coming, but the name stood and that's how the river got its name."

Billy wasn't exactly blown away by this new snippet but he did like the fact that the stream by which he stood had such a long history. It made him feel important and he believed that the stream and the meadow and the bridge would be around for many years to come yet. This settled his little mind and allowed him to relax even more; perhaps he hadn't noticed that the upheaval of moving home had actually been a rather stressful experience for him. Now that he was beginning to feel at home here, he was realising that subconsciously, it was a more traumatic experience than he had noticed. He remembered Johnny's words on the eve of the move; 'Moving is the most stressful life event – more stressful than being given a new job on the farm; more stressful than a change in lifestyle.' And he was right. When the parties stopped at Hillside Farm and the two of them had to change their habits, they both resented their new lifestyles at first. But as they began to notice their energy levels improving and the increased shine on their fur or feathers, they both realised that it was for the best. The same could be said for their new environment; it was for the best that they were here. They were together; they had their family.

As the three of them stood at the bridge, a disturbance of some kind from the island grabbed their attention. Just a gentle rustling coming from within the darkness of the treeline, but enough to make their ears prick, or in Johnny's case, his neck straighten. They watched the trees for something more but there was nothing.

"Have you ever seen the bull, dad?" asked Johnny.

"Yeah, a couple of times," he said. "Glimpses, you know; shadows and sounds rather than actual sightings. He keeps himself to himself I suppose. I know if I lived on a deserted island, I wouldn't want people staring at me all the time so I'd stay behind the treeline too."

"What's on the other side of the trees?" asked Billy.

"Well, it's a big island, Billy." said Gruff. "I doubt the bull is actually on his own over there. I mean there must be plenty of other wildlife that lives on the island. There's always birds flying across there and you never know what secrets a forest hides. I bet there are still creatures in the world that haven't been discovered yet – who knows, maybe some of them are living on that island."

They stared out over the stream and scanned the sloping verges of the island. They followed the field upwards towards the first set of trees and they froze. Johnny gave a little cluck of shock and Billy whimpered a bleat of fright as he gasped. There before them, standing at the edge of the forest was the bull, staring right back at them. Perhaps he had been there the whole time. They certainly would have noticed him appear. He was huge. He looked like a bulldozer waiting to assist on a construction site. The flat border of trees hid what was surely a massive body; only the bull's head and face could be seen. His eyes were fixed on the three watchers across the river. His bland expression gave nothing away; if anything, he seemed completely unimpressed. Unblinking, the bull exhaled a loud snort. Billy was sure he saw two streams of mist emerge from each moist nostril. Was it an angry gesture or was the bull just breathing? Was it a warning to stay away or a signal of friendship? Never before had any of them witnessed an 'I come in peace' moment but if this was it, they weren't convinced. The bull shuffled backwards into the obscurity of the woodland. Not once did he take his eyes off them. Gruff could still see his eyes glistening through the blackness before they disappeared entirely. They were alone again and they stood in silence for a moment, perhaps contemplating whether or not they had actually seen the bull. Maybe they had all been part of the same illusion; all this talk of ogres and monsters and legend had gone to their heads. But just to make them absolutely positive, another deep bellow exuded from within the trees. Billy and Johnny had had enough, both turning and scampering up the meadow to the safety of their pen. Even Gruff (who was usually so calm and unruffled, and had never run away from anything in his life) had an extra spring in his step as he quickly trotted up the slope and disappeared without fuss into his own dwelling. Oblivious to the recent encounter, and himself unperturbed by the bull's bellow, a little robin flew down and landed on one of the handrails of the bridge. The Troll's Arc creaked and the water continued to run beneath it. The bridge did not collapse and a large ogre type creature did not jump out of nowhere and gobble the robin up. Now that would be silly.

The message

"Yes, I have it," said Henry, unclipping the little strap from around his breast and releasing the parcel from his person. It wasn't a message at all; it was a package. A small package but a package nonetheless. He held it in his beak and carefully placed it into Harvey's outstretched trotters. For someone who was so caught up in his food and experimenting with different tastes, Harvey didn't make much of an effort when it came to hygiene. He was still absolutely filthy from lounging in the mud pit. He noticed Henry's perplexed look.

"What?" Harvey said. "It's clean mud, don't worry."

When Henry had been propositioned with the mission he had just completed, he assumed it was a simple case of go get it, bring it back. He couldn't fathom why Harvey had insisted upon the minimum tolerance and the free air space. He was also confused as to why Harvey had seemed so nervous; why he was so concerned with every little detail of the task. It was as though Harvey had developed an obsession with it; ever since he and his brothers had made it home safely with their father after defeating the Wolf, Harvey had become infatuated with the meticulous details of everything. Henry guessed that so well planned was their return home from their father's cave upon Springfield Mount, Harvey now left nothing to chance. If he was thinking of going for a stroll around Hillside Farm, he would check the weather forecast with Daisy the Cow (who had an unblemished record of predicting the weather, right down to the timings of when the rain would start, to the maximum or minimum temperatures for the day). Harvey would check to see if Daisy was swatting flies with her tail in a particular way, or if she was lying down on the grass to save a dry spot. 'Daisy's in a mood today; must be rain,' he'd say, after deciding not to go for that stroll after all. It wasn't that Henry was worried about Harvey – far from it. It was just that since the little pig's return from his adventure, he seemed to take life a bit more seriously, and he didn't like being kept waiting, especially when it came to preparing a banquet for an approaching event.

In this instance, the delivery that Henry had just handed over to Harvey was a small pouch of Clary Sage. Harvey had scrupulously researched the herb, identifying its precise uses and suitability. The event in question was one of great importance to him and his family and he wasn't going to leave any stone unturned in his search for perfection. The Clary Sage was an essential ingredient in a particular wine that Harvey was planning to serve, alongside a vegetable hotpot that he'd also been scouring the farm for in recent days. Harvey took the parcel and walked it over to his cooking station behind the pigsty; he motioned for Henry for follow him and indicated that he wanted to hear all about the pick-up.

"Well you know what happened on the way back with Edward," said Henry. "Up until that point, the mission was going like clockwork, just as you said. I flew over Gruff and Sally's field, which is looking lovely by the way; they're doing a very good job at looking after that meadow."

Harvey, who had been carefully unravelling the parcel of Clary Sage, stopped and looked at Henry as if to say 'get on with it.'

"Sorry. As I was saying, I flew over their little meadow, lovely, and over the Silkstream. By the way, that little bridge is looking ready to fall into the river any minute, you know…"

With a much sterner look, Harvey stared at Henry, almost spilling the contents of his treasured parcel on the floor.

"Err, yes, where was I?" stammered Henry. "Oh yes, the bridge. So I settled in the trees on the island and exactly where you said it would be, there it was. I saw it straight away. I just swooped down, gathered some up and parcelled it up for you just like that. There was no bull in sight anywhere; you were right about that too. He must have been on the other side at the time, or hidden in the forest. If you don't mind me asking, how did you know where the Clary Sage would be?"

Harvey looked again at Henry, this time with a look of self-satisfaction on his chops. He raised his right trotter and tapped it against his snout three times. "Never you mind, Henry my old friend," he said. "Never you mind." It was clear that the research Harvey had been doing was actually as scrupulous as Henry had guessed it to be. "Continue," Harvey said.

"Well, that's it," said Henry. "It really was as simple as you anticipated. After gathering up the sage, I just took off and had my little encounter with old Edward." Henry paused for a moment, watching Harvey skilfully prepare the Clary Sage, handling it with great care and placing sections of the plant into a small pan of something boiling. It already smelled amazing and the event wasn't for a couple of days yet. "Oh, I did notice some unusual tracks, though." Henry said, all of a sudden.

"Tracks?" said Harvey. "What tracks?"

"Strange ones. Certainly not bull tracks anyway. You know what that island is like. There's always some story being told about it; some nonsense," laughed Henry, nervously. "I just noticed that's all. It's probably nothing."

Harvey nodded absentmindedly, having already forgotten that Henry was talking, too absorbed in his arrangements to notice. With a roll of his eyes, Henry flapped away; no doubt off to complete some other mission of high importance.

Meanwhile, it was all kicking off in the pigsty. Harvey wasn't the only one who understood the importance of careful planning. His brothers, Davey and Stanley, were in their room, revising the talks they were about to give in a few days, going over the finer details and enquiring from each other whether or not they needed to jazz their stories up a bit with a little added fiction. They were both very confident that their stories were already full of enough courage and bravery that they needed no spicing up whatsoever. Downstairs, their parents, Jeremy and Cynthia were dancing cheek to cheek, still blissfully in love and very much excited about the up-and-coming soiree.

Oh no they didn't

That evening, as the moon shone brightly in the vast, starry sky, a goat and a cock were rustling in the grassland outside their pen, about to do something that they had promised they wouldn't do. They had spent all day talking about it. Yes, in the days following the vow they had made to Gruff, they had both been too afraid to even contemplate venturing onto the island. The bull's loud call was enough to cement that promise in stone. But with each long, sunny day, the temptation eventually became too much to bear, and the two scoundrels looked at each other earlier that morning and both knew immediately what the other was thinking. It was almost as though they had no choice in the matter. It wasn't a case of if; it was a case of when. If you're planning on doing something you shouldn't, you just need to get it done. Otherwise, it will niggle away at you for ever. You'll think or talk yourself out of it, or some do-gooder will convince you otherwise. Doing the wrong thing sometimes feels so right. Of the many conversations they had had that day, the one they had down by the river, under the glare of the afternoon sun, finalised things.

 "Spending too much time in your comfort zone isn't healthy, Billy," said Johnny. "We've got to live a little."

"I know but we made a promise," said Billy.

"Rules and promises get broken all the time," replied Johnny. "It's not as if we're putting anyone in danger."

"No, just ourselves," Billy said.

"But that's what life's about. We're young and free. If we don't do this thing, we'll regret it forever."

"I think we're gonna regret it if we *do* do it," worried Billy. He wanted to go but felt guilty about betraying his dad. This and the sheer fear of what might happen once they got over the bridge; *if* they got over the bridge.

"Remember what Harvey, Stanley and Davey all said when they returned from their adventure?" said Johnny, placing a reassuring wing around Billy's shoulder and giving him a squeeze. "They said it was the scariest and best thing they'd ever done and they wouldn't change it for the world. Look what's happened to them since they decided to leave their home. They're heroes now. We could be heroes, Billy."

"I don't know if I want to be a hero," said Billy, pulling out a tuft of grass with his hoof and chewing on it, thoughtfully.

"Look, are we going or not?" asked Johnny, getting slightly impatient with Billy's inability to make a decision.

"Yes, we're going," said Billy, catching Johnny off guard with his assertiveness. "We're going and we're going tonight." Billy never needed any convincing. He knew that he and Johnny were going, he just didn't want to admit it to himself; he couldn't commit to it, not this early in the day. But the decision had been made, and he'd made it. Perhaps Johnny was glad that they were going. Perhaps Johnny was just glad that he hadn't had the final say; if it all went wrong, it was Billy who actually said that they were going, not Johnny. Sometimes it's a lot easier to go along with something if you haven't had to make any of the decisions, if none of the responsibility is yours.

They had spent the afternoon trying not to be too obvious that they were planning something, but they just couldn't help themselves. It was fortunate that Sally had calmed down a little after Johnny's recent confession and they were on a much looser leash. Despite this, they tried their best to behave as inconspicuously as possible. For two young jokers who would usually spend all day playing in the grass, it would have been clear to anyone who was paying the slightest bit of attention that these two were up to something. One minute, instead of running around the field as usual, they were in deep, hushed conversation, lying down low in one shady corner of the meadow. The next minute, rather than entertaining the school children at the fence in the afternoon, they were nowhere to be seen, whispering in their pen and readying themselves to put their plan into action. Gruff and Sally were too trusting and too relaxed in their perfect meadow to notice these obvious changes in behaviour. Even when Sally pointed out that the school children were at the fence, Gruff just nodded and dismissed it, noting that it would do the little blighters good to miss out on something for a change. And when Gruff took his evening stroll down to the water's edge, he noticed that the field was unusually quiet. If he had put two and two together he may have found the pair of them, craftily tightening Billy's bell, so that it wouldn't clink or clank as he walked.

The night time was always a noisy affair in the countryside. Yes, the peace and quiet was deafening, but if one stood and listened for a while, one would notice just how busy it can get in the dark. Sound seems to travel well in the still air of the night and noises from miles away can seem to be coming from behind the nearest tree. Even the sound of a gentle snap of a tiny twig underfoot, one that wouldn't be heard during the day, can be magnified in the quiet of nightfall, to the point that it literally echoes off the leaves. This night was no different. As soon as their little heads appeared through the entrance to their pen, Billy and Johnny's task suddenly seemed all the more terrifying. It was pitch black but the light of the moon seemed to act as a huge torch in the night sky, illuminating everything. It was only a short distance down the mound of the meadow to the bridge but at that moment, it seemed miles away. The sound of running water was never even noticed during the day but this evening, it sounded like the water was high up the sides of the riverbanks and charging downstream in a torrent.

Carefully, ever so carefully, they stepped out into the bright darkness of the meadow and began to slowly edge their way down towards the stream. Gruff could be heard snoring loudly through the walls of the pen, making it seem as though he was actually sleeping right outside in the open air. Of course, he wasn't; he was fast asleep, tucked up in bed and from previous experience, it was going to take a lot to wake him up. Fortunately for Billy and Johnny, their parents were both very deep sleepers; the country air had a lot to do with it as well, even though they had all spent their entire lives in the country, it didn't stop them from commenting every now and then just how deeply the country air made them sleep. One hoof in front of the other; one claw placed down after each awkward strut. Never a more comical sight to be seen; a goat and a rooster sneaking down the slope of a meadow, intent on crossing a rickety old bridge to investigate the personality of an aggressive and bothersome bull on the other side. Before they knew it, they were stood at the edge of Troll's Arc.

"Why is it called Troll's Arc, again?" whispered Johnny.

"Shut up!" snapped Billy, angrily. For a split second he'd forgotten where they were and his voice seemed loud in the open air. The goat and the rooster had to duck down and look around to see if they had disturbed anything.

All remained still and, possibly to their disappointment, all remained clam. They were clear to attempt the crossing of Troll's Arc.

Not just another evening

In the days leading up to an event at Hillside Farm, there was always a lot of work to do. The campsite area had to be prepared; seats for the guests and kindling for the fire. This was Stanley's job. He had a keen eye for the right sort of wood or bark; not that they needed much. The fire was just for show, to add a bit of atmosphere to their storytelling. The guests, in their thick coats or warm feathers, were used to being outside at night and never usually relied on a fire to keep them warm. Even on one occasion in early May, when Teddy the sheep had just been sheared, his huge woolly overcoat gone, he was completely comfortable sitting around through the rather chilly night, listening to his hosts describe their adventures. With just the embers of a small fire crackling away, it was more likely to be Harvey's spiced mulled wine that had kept him warm. Davey, who had a particular eye for detail when it came to organising the theme for the night, would liaise with his family to discuss who the guests were for each event and then create a personalised atmosphere just for them. If their guests were particularly fussy, Davey would pull out all the stops to create a pristine and well organised surrounding, but if the pigs were expecting a more relaxed visitor, the bales of hay would be a little more broken up, enabling them to relax and lounge a little more. Harvey was obviously responsible for providing the cuisine for the evening and Cynthia would always like to assist with stirring or suggesting. Harvey allowed her the freedom to stir and suggest but nothing more, the cooking was his domain and everybody knew it.

Jeremy would prepare for the evening with a long soak in the mud pit and a stroll around Hillside Farm. It was his job to make sure that everything was just as it should be. The last thing they wanted was for something to happen that required Farmer George's attention. Creatures would pay a hefty sum to be wined and dined by the piglets and they didn't want to be interrupted by an interfering farmer, turning up unexpectedly right in the middle of one of Davey's stories. So Jeremy would walk around the farm and visit all the animals, reminding everyone that there would be an event that evening and that he expected everything to run like clockwork. They all chipped in; whenever there was an event, Farmer George's job seemed very simple. He would sometimes find himself scratching his head at how tidy all the bedding areas were, or how all the feed stations were fully stocked. Of course, throughout the day, little did he know that all the animals on the farm, even his trusty dog, Ron, had been working hard to make sure everything was in place.

At the campsite, which was located in a secluded area just behind the pigsty, everything was nearly ready for the forthcoming entertainment. It was never a case of throwing a few things together on the day; the entire family played their part and it was normal for each of them to be busy for perhaps a week prior to the finishing touches being done. With just a matter of days of preparation left, Harvey had been slaving away at the stove, making sure to return to his mud pit whenever George did his rounds. Stanley had collected enough kindling (cedar bark, dry leaves and twigs) and tinder (dry grasses and birch tree bark) to last them well into the early hours, if needed. Davey had set the scene, scattering daisy flower heads about the floor and placing the hay bales a safe distance from the fire, but close enough to create the right atmosphere. Of course, there was a slightly raised area from which the storytelling could take place. Davey was specific about this and insisted upon it being slightly raised; he said that it meant the audience would have to look up at the performers from below. It created the illusion that the pigs were heroic and the stories were even more remarkable in reality than they sounded, despite the expert way in which they were retold. Without doubt, any creature who has heard the tale of the adventure in question, will confirm that the pigs were indeed heroes and the stories were certainly remarkable. Such was the atmosphere that could be created at these retellings, guests would have to reminded to leave the farm quietly, so as not to disturb Farmer George and spoil the perfect set up they had going. The overhanging trees sealed the area like the roof of a theatre, but allowed stars to be seen through gaps in the leaves, creating a magical setting. Birds and other small creatures would come to marvel at the little auditorium; two robins spent the morning playing in the branches, quickly dropping down to ground level to steal away with some of Stanley's kindle wood, which was perfect for their little nest. Meanwhile, a pair of squirrels would take it turns to scamper down the trunk of their current tree and dart through the middle of the camp, just as one of the pigs was about to return, effectively playing chicken. Not that any of the organisers would have shooed them away; small creatures such as these were welcomed and encouraged to attend the evenings in question. Davey saw it as free advertising; the robins would already have told a couple of their friends about a cool place to pick up some materials for nest buildings and the chatty little squirrels, who were always up to mischief, would definitely have boasted about their acts of bravery to other creatures of the forest. Even the insects played their part and whenever the pigs were reciting their feats of courage to paying guests, the whole theatre would be packed full of little beady eyes, blinking and twinkling as they watched. The branches would be full of tiny spectators, lined up carefully so as not to fall. The leaves would droop with the weight of slugs and caterpillars, all intent on getting the best seats in the house.

Already, a few days before the big night, if one looked very closely, one could make out the movements of thousands of different insects from all over the countryside, arriving early like holidaymakers keen to grab the best poolside sun loungers early in the morning. An army of ants marched up the trunk of one of smaller trees, moving everything in its path out of its way. Cries of objection rang out as anything else on the tree was pushed out of the way by the onslaught of the ants. There was plenty of room, however, and even a small hummingbird and his family, who would usually feast hungrily on such a number of ants, contently hovered over to another branch. Despite the ants, there was generally a good atmosphere and many of the insects spent the time chatting away, reminiscing of Cynthia's infamous parties, and more recently, the nights of entertainment that they were all here to witness once again. It wasn't as if they had all turned up to watch something they'd seen before. This wasn't as straight forward as a stand-up comedian delivering the same content night after night to different audiences. Each of these occasions were unique; there was always something new to be heard in the stories that were told, there was always some new-fangled item on the menu that Harvey would have been raving about in the days leading up to the big night. The insects and other small creatures saw it as a not-to-be-missed addition to the calendar. It wasn't as if the pigs could charge everybody for attending – it would have been pandemonium to control an audience of that size. It made more sense to allow those who could sneak in 'unnoticed' to do just that; their presence at these events always added to the atmosphere and the pigs were glad to have as many enthusiasts watching down on them as they could fit in the heights of the trees.

The gate crashers not only added to the ambience of the evening, just by being there, they also had a few other uses; as they watched, some of the insects would glow or twinkle in the moonlight, adding to the starry, starry night effect. In addition, by the time the paying guests were gone, the onlookers would feast on the crumbs and other leftovers, basically saving the pigs a major tidy-up job before Farmer George did his rounds in the morning. In the commotion that was usually created, the ashes of the fire would be flapped or blown away and any evidence of revelry would be picked up by birds looking to add to their nests. Even more obscure items that had been discarded, such as a hand-crafted novelty straw, or some other little decoration that Cynthia had taken the time to put up, were whisked away to be kept as mementos of the experience. Something to say 'I was there.'

Cynthia was very much looking forward to spending the evening with Sally, Gruff and the kids, and she had been in fine spirits all week, spring cleaning the house and ordering Jeremy around whenever it looked as though he was about to head out to the mud pit. As much as he loved bathing in the slurp, there was nothing that made him happier than working with Cynthia, doing things as a couple. Since his return to the farm, their life together had been so lovely; they had learnt the power of communication and understanding, and how important these things were in a working relationship. Henry had been deployed a few days earlier to message the guests that their booking had been confirmed and that they were expected for arrival-cocktails at 9pm sharp. At that time, George and Mary would be enjoying their usual cup of cocoa before bed and, unless something completely out of the ordinary occurred, they wouldn't be venturing out of their cosy little farmhouse until the following morning. Everything was running like clockwork; the animals on the farm were making as little mess as possible, thereby giving Farmer George almost nothing to do other than drive his tractor from field to field. Each time he got to a new field, the grass was in good condition, the extra feed troughs were well stocked and the animals were happily snoozing or playing quietly. It almost made him suspicious.

"I could have sworn that trough was half empty earlier today," he'd say to himself, pulling gently at his beard. "Oh well, one less thing to do." And off he would go, on to the next field, where he would have exactly the same conversation with himself all over again. But what could he get suspicious about? His beautiful farm was pretty much running itself; it just made him think that he and Mary must have been such a good team and must have been doing such a great job. After all, it wasn't as if his animals were hiding something from him; it wasn't as if they were all working together for some greater purpose. Obviously, the thought never crossed his mind, not even once. He would have to be mad to think that now wouldn't he?

Oh yes they did

"I'll go first," whispered Billy. "If it can take my weight, you'll be fine." With the moon behind him in the sky, the shadow of his horns stretched out across Troll's Arc like two curved swords, poised to slice a pathway into the unknown. Johnny watched, crouching at the first handrail of the bridge, observing intensely as Billy placed his right hoof carefully onto the bridge. It creaked loudly and he quickly removed it, stepping backwards onto the soft grass. They looked at each other and Johnny nodded encouragingly.

"Trust the bridge, Billy," he said.

"That's easy for you to say," replied Billy, cautiously moving towards the bridge once more. The same creaks echoed around the field again as Billy stepped out, a little more determined, but a little more gently. Johnny looked back over his left shoulder at the pen on top of the mound to check if anything was stirring. Nothing was stirring; he could still make out Gruff's faint snoring through the walls. Another step, another creaking wrench from the bridge, as Billy boldly eased onward over the dilapidated slats. As the groaning bridge continued to support his weight, he grew in confidence and kept his momentum going, one foot in front of the other. As he looked down, he could see the water running beneath him through the laths and a shiver went through his spine. What if it collapsed and he fell in? Could he even swim? Placing his feet as widely as he could, trying to keep his burden on the bridge away from the centre of the boards, Billy found himself just a few more steps away from the other side. Not that this was much of a reassurance; on the other side of the bridge awaited an angry and powerful bull, which would probably not take too kindly to being disturbed in the middle of the night. Resisting the urge to leap to so-called safety, Billy edged forward as smoothly as possible and upon making it to the other side, turned triumphantly to his buddy who was watching open-beaked and wide-eyed.

Now it was Johnny's turn. Rushing slightly, his wattle wobbling around like a deflated balloon, Johnny strutted clumsily across the bridge. His sharp toe nails dug into the planks, leaving little holes as they were pulled out; evidence that a cock had braved the crossing of Troll's Arc. And those little holes made it all the way across, a long line of footprints marking his achievement forever like a tagging of graffiti. He strutted onto the island proudly, the blade of his comb flapping side to side as he and Billy celebrated silently together, unaware that they were being watched the whole time. Two beady eyes sat in the darkness of the trees above a black, glistening nose and two open nostrils, which breathed silently in and out.

"What do we do now?" asked Johnny, as they cowered together in the tall grasses.

Billy scanned the tree line, much in the same way as he had done the other day when his father had made him promise never to do what he now in the process of doing. Noticing a slight gap in the trees, he gestured with his head and began strolling up towards the wood. A second pair of eyes appeared in the hidden woodland, next to the first; and then a third. Three pairs of eyes; six evil green marbles, seemingly suspended in mid air and fixed on the newcomers below. Half way up the slope, exactly between the bridge and the supposed safety of the wood, Johnny and Billy froze. A rustle of some kind from above the ridge stopped them in their tracks. They were unaware of the six eyes that watched them from their hiding place, but this wasn't where the rustle came from. Their attention was fully fixed on the clearing towards which they were initially headed. The moon still sat high in the sky, providing a perfect backdrop for the scene that began to unfold in front of their eyes. On the crest of the ridge, a dark figure loomed. Slowly, a silhouette began to form and the two intruders watched in terror as the outline of an enormous bull's head emerged in the moonlight. Two gigantic horns arched towards each other and as the bull stepped slowly over the ridge, his true size became clearer; he was immense. Steam rose off his back, which heaved in and out with every breath and his giant hooves shook the ground, even though he was only walking slowly.

But he didn't walk slowly for very long. Billy and Johnny looked at each other as the bull began to step forward with a little more purpose in his stride. The uninvited duo edged backwards, almost falling over each other on the uneven slants of the hill. Unnoticed, the three pairs of eyes began to appear from the tree line on the right. The bull broke out into an immediate sprint, going from almost zero to full speed remarkably quickly for an animal of his size. Johnny turned on his hocks, and was gone in a flash, down the hill towards the bridge. He turned to see Billy right behind him; Billy had also shown good reactions and he too moved remarkably quickly. His incentive was clear to see. The bull pounded down the hill, closing on the escaping pair and he wasn't slowing. Still unseen, the six green eyes were also making their way downhill through the darkness, verging upon the goat and rooster with great speed themselves. Closer the apparent safety of the bridge became, closer still the thunderous pounding of the bull's relentless gallop sounded in their ears. He powered down the hill, gaining with every step, his huge mass and the gradient of the slope enabling him to reach unheard of speeds of up to 40mph. Goats and roosters can't run anywhere near that quickly. Down the middle of the slope came Billy and Johnny, pursued from their left by the massive beast. They never had a chance to spot the cunning eyes that also approached from their right.

Nearer to the bridge they got, gasping for air out of sheer panic. Smaller still became the gap between them and their chasers. As they approached the raggedy wooden structure, the shadow of the bull loomed ever closer behind them. Together, they sprinted across the bridge, without care for its stability. Johnny's wings flapped wildly as he tried his best to get across to the safety of the meadow. Billy sprinted alongside him and this time, he did leap. He leapt with all his might, soaring through the air and landing in a crumpled heap on the soft grass. The bridge moaned, the same as before, but it didn't budge. It held fast. The bull skidded to an abrupt halt right at the foot of the bridge. As soon as the three pairs of eyes had the goat and the cock make it over the bridge to safety, they turned and were gone as quickly as they emerged. The three that were left looked at one another over the derelict structure and all became immediately calm; even their breathing seemed to recover. It was almost as though the bull had them in a trance, its hypnotic stare preventing Billy or Johnny from moving or even from looking away. For what seemed like an eternity, they stood in a stand off. Perhaps there was a legend from the time of cowboys that told of a similar Wild West style situation across this very bridge. If there were, it would not have been as tense a standoff as this one. The moon was still high in the sky, lighting the stage below it, as though it was the final scene of an epic movie and the main characters were about to settle things once and for all. But even that would not have had the same intensity that could be felt in this unlikely location, on this otherwise unremarkable night.

After a long moment, perhaps not quite the eternity it seemed, but long enough nonetheless, the bull snorted a steamy and misty snort. With a swish of his tail, he turned to leave but not before he gave Billy one final stare. It was a stare that made a connection; a stare that made Billy think. It wasn't an angry look or an aggressive look. It was as though the bull was trying to communicate with Billy. Johnny didn't notice; he was too preoccupied with inspecting all his faculties to check that he was still in one piece. His feathers were ruffled and the points of his comb atop his crown were flattened and misshaped. His main sickles were tangled amongst his saddle and he took a moment to pluck, shake, pull and tug at the necessary places to make himself presentable once again. Still mesmerised by the bull's stare, Billy remained sure footed, his barrel of a chest heaving deeply as he took a sigh of relief that he was back on familiar ground. His tail needed a quick fluffing after the tumble he took and he rubbed his muzzle in the grass, taking in the scents of his beloved meadow.

"Not a word about this to…" Billy attempted to say.

"Billy!" came a shout from the mound. Gruff was running down the gentle slope towards his children with a concerned and anxious look on his face. "What's going on?" The youngsters just stood there, looking at their feet. This time, Gruff did put two and two together and realised exactly what was going on. "You went over to the island, didn't you?" he demanded.

Billy was just about to object when Johnny blurted out. "Yes! We're sorry! The bull is crazy! He was going to kill us!" Johnny was frantic, strutting up and down, flapping his wings almost as wildly as he did when he was practically flying across the bridge just moments ago. "We couldn't resist, but you were right, Dad! That bull is dangerous!"

"OK, calm down," said Gruff. "You'll wake your mother."

"I'm already awake," said Sally from inside her pen. "And you two are grounded. Indefinitely!" her voice sounded muffled, coming through the walls of her shelter but Billy and Johnny could tell that she was cross. None of the other night-time noises could be heard; mainly because they weren't being listened to. All the usual noises were still going on in the background but the three individuals in the open field were too concerned with their current situation. Gruff was angry and disappointed that his children had disobeyed him; even though he understood that they both had adventurous streaks in them, he had hoped that his warning would have been enough. Johnny was almost relieved that he'd got the burden of their promise breaking off his chest and he was thankful that he and Billy had made it back form that island in one piece. Billy didn't show it but he was furious with Johnny for revealing the truth to their father, without thinking even for second. And so soon after the little man-to-man talk they'd had about this very topic. But Billy was also thinking about the bull. Not about how huge he was or how scary he was; Billy was thinking about the look the bull gave him before he turned his back on him. He still couldn't put his hoof on it. Did it make him feel uneasy? Or did it make him feel inquisitive? Either way, he would have time to mull all this over for the next few days at least while he was grounded. He would also have time to get to the bottom of things with Johnny, regarding how quickly he shouted his mouth off before thinking of the consequences. That cock still had a lot to learn.

"Go to bed," said Gruff, pointing sternly to their kidding pen.

Billy's return

The next day went slowly for the mischievous explorers. Neither of them had slept particularly well, following the incident the night before; Billy had spent most of the night thinking about the bull and Johnny had tossed and turned, feeling bad about how their actions had upset Gruff and Sally so much. It was a very sombre mood on the meadow and Gruff and Sally did their best to make sure that the goat and rooster knew they were in the doghouse. Gruff wasn't there for the usual morning stroll along the strait; there were no interesting chats and intriguing facts for the children to be entertained by. Everybody seem to be keeping themselves to themselves and to say that Billy and Johnny were getting the cold shoulder treatment was an understatement. As the seconds ticked by slowly and the minutes seemed to drag on one at a time, Billy took the opportunity to have some alone time; to reflect on the previous night's events and to ponder his next move. Johnny was certainly near the top of his to do list and Billy spent a full hour contemplating how he was going to break it to him gently that Johnny was going to have to toughen up. Despite his obvious outgoing personality and his adventurous side, Johnny was a sensitive soul and Billy was right to give this careful consideration. The last thing he wanted was to fall out with his best friend, but if they were going to continue their jaunts out of the perimeter of the meadow (over the bridge or fence), things were going to have to change. As he watched a busy robin, diligently pulling a long worm out of the mud of the riverbank, Billy decided that he would speak to Johnny later that day. The robin flew away in the direction of Hillside Farm and Billy starred into space for a moment, simply resting in the calming field.

Another priority near the very top of his to do list was the bull. Billy still had many unanswered questions whirling around his head and that look the bull had given him stuck in his mind, clear as a freshly shaken polaroid. There was something in his eyes, Billy recalled, that didn't feel right; it wasn't the look of an animal that was hell bent on killing them. If the bull had set out down that slope with the intention of running Billy and Johnny through, of trampling them until they breathed their last breaths, surely the bull would have reacted in a different way. Surely he would have been angry that he failed to catch them and would have given out another one of his tremendous bellows to warn them of his feelings. So calm and unmoved was the bull, once the goat and the rooster had made it over the bridge to safety, it was almost as though the bull was glad or relieved. This didn't make any sense at all to Billy and he knew that this would also require a lot of mulling over. He slowly chewed a thick, lush clump of grass and looked at the water flowing downstream.

Lunch was always a chance for the family to spend some quality time together. Although all they really ate was the grass in the meadow, Sally usually took the time create a little area in which they all sat, choosing a different part of the field each time. This not only prevented things from getting dull, it also ensured that different sections of grass were grazed each day. It was the main reason why the meadow was in such good condition and why the grass grew so well there. Today's lunch was an awkward affair, as there was little talk and a frosty atmosphere. Sally looked sternly at her children as they played with their selected tussocks, and Gruff chewed pensively as he considered the severity of the punishment that had been bestowed upon the children.

"So," began Sally, making up Gruff's mind for him, "while your father and I are visiting Jeremy and Cynthia, you two are to stay inside your pen and I don't want any mischief. We are very disappointed that you both ignored your father's instructions. We want you to be safe and we expect you to listen to our rules. When you have your own meadows to tend to, you can make the rules but until then, you'll do as your told."

Well and truly put in their place, Billy and Johnny kept

their heads down and just nodded slightly in response to the doe's lambast. Despite being a sweet, loving mother, Sally was also strict and had always had high expectations when it came to the attitudes and behaviour of her children. Billy and Johnny had been raised to be polite and respectful to all creatures and it was clear that they had overstepped the mark this time.

"We'll be spending a few hours with Jeremy and Cynthia," Gruff said, "so it will give you both a chance to think about your behaviour. Last night, you let me down, you let your mother down, but most importantly, you let yourselves down. We expect to hear nothing more about the bull and we certainly don't want to find out that either of you have gone over there again. Not only is that bridge ready to fall into the river at any minute, that bull is very dangerous. Just imagine it collapsed while you were over there last night; you would have been trapped and your mother and I might have lost you forever." Gruff was really laying the guilt trip on thick and as Sally wiped a solitary tear from her eye, he finished with, "I do not want you to disobey myself or your mother again."

There was no double-checking, this time, that the young duo had heard what had been said to them, no further reminders of the consequences; their parents had spoken and there was nothing more to be said on the matter. Without speaking, once they had finished their lunch, Billy and Johnny slunk away to their pen and spent the remainder of the afternoon sulking and moping about. Billy took the opportunity to tick off one of the items on his list to do. Johnny's inability to remain calm and basically keep his mouth shut when it mattered had got them into trouble twice in recent days, and Billy had the feeling that, unless a clear-the-air talk was had, it could turn into an on-going issue.

"Johnny, we could have got away with it if you hadn't have told Dad that we'd been across the bridge last night," Billy said. "Dad had no way of knowing that we had been to the island and we could be on our way to see Stanley, Harvey and Davey. You know how much we like Harvey's cooking, and I was looking forward to hearing more about their adventure to Springfield Mount."

"I know, Billy," Johnny replied. "I was just freaked out about nearly being killed by that bull and I couldn't help myself. As soon I saw Dad coming down the hill, I just thought it was best to come clean. He must have known we were up to something when he caught us out in the field in the middle of the night."

"Yes, but he didn't actually see us on the island and if you'd just taken a minute to think, we could have told him that we were thinking of going over there but we had changed our minds," said Billy. "He probably would have commended us for making a good decision. And, while we're on the subject, why did you tell mum about the camomile tea at Cynthia's parties? There was no need to make her worry about all that stuff. It's in the past and what she doesn't know about it won't upset her.

You know how she worries about us."

"I just got caught up in the moment. It just slipped out," said Johnny, opening his wings in a pleading, forgive me gesture.

"OK, but from now on, you've got to think before you speak. Yes, it's important that we're honest, but sometimes, it's good to keep your cards close to your chest."

The two of them sat together in silence for a long reflective moment.

"I know I messed up'" said Johnny. "It won't happen again. The next time I sense the urge to blurt something out, I'll remember to take a deep breath and think about what I'm going to say."

"All right, good," said Billy, extending a hoof in Johnny's direction. "Let's shake on it."

Johnny's wing entwined itself around Billy's hoof and the two of them shook on it, looking at each other as they did. The mood inside the pen was lifted and even though they were disappointed not to be going to Hillside Farm for the soiree of the century, they were both happy to have had the talk and Billy was confident that Johnny had learnt his lesson. Whether or not he'd be able to keep his mouth shut the next time a similar situation arose remained to be seen.

The children on their way home from school that afternoon skipped and shouted their way to the usual spot at the fence of the meadow. As they waited excitedly for the appearance of Billy and Johnny, they played pat-a-cake and called out to their would-be entertainers. The goat and the rooster would usually make them laugh, horsing around and strutting their stuff. But today, there was no Billy, acting the giddy goat and they were barking up the wrong tree if they thought they'd get as much as a cock-a-doodle-doo out of the rooster. Instead, Billy and Johnny were lacklustre and uninspiring. The children watched them both as they trudged over to gate, their heads low and their demeanours quite the opposite to their usually energetic state. The two groups met at the fence and stared at each other, waiting. The children looked at the animals, expecting some kind of reaction and the animals stared back, as if to suggest that maybe it could be the turn of the children to play the entertainers. As if some weird form of telekinetic communication had taken place, that's exactly what happened. The four children began pulling faces at the glum creatures; not in a cruel way, but in a jovial and happy manner. Blowing raspberries and sticking their tongues out, they could almost sense a change in the behaviour of the animals and one of the children even thought to herself that she saw the goat smile. The enthusiastic youngsters, swinging their school bags around their heads and jumping over them like skipping ropes, certainly had a positive impact on the miserable twosome and as they left, Johnny gave out call of gratitude that made the entire group whoop and shout with joy. His cock-a-doodle-doo was clear and loud, and rang through the countryside, awakening anyone or anything in the vicinity from his or her mid-afternoon siestas.

But it didn't change anything as far as Billy and Johnny were concerned. They were still in trouble with their parents and they were still banished from going to the party. Billy lay down in his pen and reflected further on the on-going situations. He'd had his chat with Johnny and felt that it had worked to clear the air a little between them. It was one thing less to do on his to do list anyway, and he felt better about that at least. The bull on the island was completely another matter and one that would need careful evaluation.

As night time fell upon the tranquil meadow, the stars twinkled and the moon sat proudly once again in the sheer black sky. The heavy emotion of the day had made Johnny tired and he snored contently next to Billy as the young kid lay, staring at the wall of his pen house. The crickets cricketed and the other nocturnal creatures of the night could be heard; the occasional rustle of bushes or crunch of twigs. Billy didn't flinch at any of it. He was deep in thought, almost in a trance. Was he actually there, contemplating another visit to the bridge and the subsequent horrors that awaited him on the other side? Was he really going to disobey his father's instructions once more? Getting caught again would surely be the end of him; Gruff would lose all trust and faith in his young son, Sally would be furious and punish him with yet more curfews, and Johnny would likely never speak to his best friend again. Another hour passed as Billy continued to weigh up the pros and cons. The list of cons was endless. The reasons against venturing out of the safety of his hutch were real and meaningful; the consequences of getting caught dire. But he just couldn't shake it out of his mind. That look the bull gave him was etched firmly into his mind. Whether his eyes were open or closed, he could still see it, plain as day.

So if he lay there for the rest of the night, considering his options, until the sun rose and a new day began, Billy knew that he would regret it; he knew that that image of the bull would never go away. Billy blinked once, and twice. He took a long, slow, deep breath in and eased it out of his little body until there was no air left inside him. He tried to visualise the process of meeting the bull but every time his imagination allowed him to leave the pen, he went blank. Billy continued to breathe and blink. He was wide awake, despite the stressful day he'd had, despite the worry and anxiety he and Johnny had caused. Despite the lopsided list of cons against pros, he got up and walked out into the meadow. He wasn't concerned about stepping on a twig or in a divot of some kind. He paid no attention to the snoring coming from his mother and father's room. He walked purposefully down the slope towards the bridge. He remembered one of his dad's talks, when the old goat was talking about life. He recalled the wise words...

'Decisions have to be made, Son. One way or the other, it's better to make a decision than to stay on the fence. The fence is an uncomfortable place and you're better off either side of it.'

Well Billy had listened. And he had made a decision. And he was acting on that decision. And he intended to see it through. Billy strode across that bridge without hesitation; as if it was made of steel. Ignoring the creaks and groans, he marched across to the other side and stood there, breathing calmly. He could hear his heart beating and he could feel the adrenaline pumping through his body. But he remained composed. He scanned the treeline above, much in the same way as he had done the last time he was here. As he looked, he felt as if he was being watched. Not from the meadow; it may have given him some peace of mind to know that his dad was watching. Billy felt eyes were on him. And they were; six of them, together in the darkness, still and unblinking, the same as before. Billy didn't see them. But he did see the same silhouette begin to emerge from the break in the trees; the shadow of the rounded horns, followed by the huge bulk of the rest of the beast. Bravely, because he was absolutely terrified, Billy stepped towards the beast and the two mammals moved forwards, the bull walking down the slope and Billy walking up it.

There was no bellow, no charge. The bull simply trudged down the hill, approaching Billy with gentle steps. The little goat was dwarfed by the enormous animal and as they came face to face, their eyes met and the mist of their breaths merged in front of them. Billy did everything he could to prevent himself from turning and sprinting home. His little heart continued to beat furiously in his chest as he stood before this legendary foe and looked right back at him as if the two animals were evenly matched. And then the bull spoke.

"You are a brave little goat." His voice was soft and soothing. "It is very dangerous for you to be here. You should have listened to your father." Billy continued to stare back at the bull, remaining silent. "This island is no place for a defenceless, young goat such as yourself."

"I don't understand," said the goat. "Why did you chase us the last time we were here? And why didn't you chase me this time?"

"You are in great danger," spoke the bull. "I am not the only one who lives on this island. Yes, it is my island but I share it with a small pack of wolves, who would to eat you up if they were able to." For the first time, Billy averted his eyes from the bull's stare and scanned the treeline once more. As the moon behind him shone luminously, his gaze fell upon a sparkling within the secrets of the trees. His head stopped still and he squinted slightly to focus. "Yes," said the bull, noticing Billy's realisation that he was indeed being watched. "You see them don't you, in the trees?"

Billy nodded slowly; six star-like twinkles hovering among the tree trunks. "Yes," he said.

"Then now you know why I chased you last night," explained the bull. "Not to catch you, but to chase you away. You didn't notice them then, but they were nearly upon you before you made it back across the bridge."

"Then why didn't they just cross the bridge if they want to eat us so badly?" asked Billy, returning his stare once more back to the bull.

"The wolves and I have an understanding," said the bull, seeming to relax in the knowledge that the little goat was beginning to believe him. He settled on the grass and Billy also lay down next to the giant creature. "We co-exist on this island, in the understanding that they stay on the island. They are an angry and resentful group who, since coming here out of the blue a few months ago, have pretty much terrorised the whole area. All sorts of animals live on this island. It was a beautiful, peaceful place until they arrived. But since they turned up, everyone lives in fear that they will be next on their list for dinner. But if they were to cross the bridge, it would mean the whole countryside would have to live in the same fear. They are the children of a once-fearsome Wolf who used to live in the mountains. You may have heard of the story of the piglets who went off in search of their estranged father, Jeremy, I think his name was."

Billy nodded eagerly. "Yes, yes! I am good friends with the pigs and I used to live on their farm!"

"Ssshhh!" the bull hushed Billy, extending a gigantic hoof in front of the little goat's mouth. "If the wolves work out exactly who you are, I may not be able to convince them to stay here – their desire to exact revenge on the pigs, and anyone they know, may just be too much of a temptation for them." The bull breathed out, shaking his monstrous head. "You are indeed an interesting little chap. You're safe with me; they won't touch you while I am here. I have told them that they must behave if they want to stay on this island. Nature shall run its course; they need to eat, but I will not allow them to unnecessarily terrorise the other animals. Until now, they have lived reasonably well and they seem happy to remain here, for the foreseeable future at least. But the minute they realise who you are, and that you're connected to the pigs all that will surely end. Those dastardly wolves will be over the bridge and into your homes quicker than you can say hold your horses."

The look that the bull had given Billy the other night was beginning to make sense. It was a look of trust, anger and almost relief. It was a look that said 'don't come back.' It was a look that said 'I'm glad you're safe, for now.' Billy and the bull sat together for a long moment in silence, allowing Billy the chance to reflect on the conversation and to realise that he had calmed down a great deal compared to when he stood face to face with the beast moments before. The bull remained still, breathing slowly and glancing up the slope to the treeline where he could make out six glistening gem-like shapes, blinking in the darkness. Then, in the blink of an eye, they vanished. The forest returned to normal, giving nothing away about the mysteries it held within.

"I have to go," said Billy. "I have to get back before Johnny knows I've gone."

"Ah," mused the bull. "Johnny must be your rooster friend. He will be interested to learn the news, I'm sure."

"Yes, but if I tell him I came back, he might never speak to me again."

"If your friendship is strong enough, he will understand," spoke the bull, all of a sudden, seeming all wise and philosophical. "Remember that these wolves are seeking revenge for what happened to their father. I can only convince them to stay on this island for so long. If they remain unaware of precisely who you are, then hopefully they will learn to live with what has happened. Hopefully they will accept things as they are and settle on the island permanently. As long as that bridge remains standing, there's always a chance that something could trigger their appetites for retribution."

"Then why doesn't somebody just knock it down?" asked Billy, buoyantly.

"That bridge has stood for hundreds of years. Some say thousands," stated the bull. "It is a very historical and important part of this landscape. Besides, how will I get across when the time comes for me to leave here?" The bull smiled, indicating that he had no intention to leave the island and that he was just pulling the goat's leg.

Billy realised this and had two reactions; disappointment that his great idea, which could have solved everyone's problem, wasn't such a great idea after all, and relief that the bull would always be there, no matter what. "I'm glad you're here," he said. "What's your name?"

"Just call me Bull," said Bull, and he heaved himself up and sauntered back up the slope. As Billy watched him go, it seemed as though the silhouette, although the same size and stature, was a lot less terrifying than before. It was almost reassuring. Billy remembered that the only thing keeping him safe on the island was disappearing over the ledge and he was now alone in the dark, at the mercy of the wolves. Quick a flash, he was up and darting across the bridge, back up to the security of his pen. As he silently entered his room, Johnny still sleeping soundly, Billy thought to himself that each time he crossed that bridge, he seemed to do so with more confidence. It was as though the rickety old structure, which had lasted the test of time among other things, was stronger than it looked. Maybe there was something magical about it. Maybe the stories about it were true. Maybe the beast that used to live beneath it actually existed. Or maybe that was all just a load of old bull.

The wolves

Many moons ago, before the goats had moved to the meadow, the Troll's Arc bore the weight of yet another group of guests. Three young and tired wolves had tested the sturdiness of that bridge, much in the same way as every other visitor had done in the past. Much in the same way as Billy had done when he first stepped out onto the creaking slats. And the result was still the same. Despite the groaning of the bridge, there was no splitting of timbers and no crashing into the stream below. The wolves were dishevelled and hungry. They had been through a dreadful ordeal and were in search of somewhere safe to lay their weary heads. Their father, the Wolf, who until recently had commanded the respect of the entire countryside, had been defeated by a boar and as the story had been told, his beaten body had been thrown over the cliffs of Wakeman's Hill. The wolves, who at the time of the epic encounter had been held captive by three nasty little pigs and had witnessed the whole thing. They had been forced to watch and once their father had been disposed of, they were unceremoniously released from their entanglements and set free into the wild with nothing. No father, no food, and in their eyes, no hope.

Their upbringing had been one of luxury and gluttony. The Wolf had provided for them in the only way he knew how; with the dead bodies of the various animals he'd killed from around the countryside, upon which, each little wolf could feast to his heart's content. They became so complacent and reliant on their father's care that they were pretty useless at fending for themselves. They had never had the need to. Until that fateful day upon the ridge of Wakeman's Hill, when they saw him tumbling down the cliff side and disappear into Silkstream River.

Shocked and confused, lost and frightened, the wolves had to learn how to defend themselves, and learn quickly. The pigs had thrust them out into the wilderness without a care for their safety or well-being. And rightly so; many of those who have heard the story have stated that the pigs were generous in their acts and would have been better off throwing the wolves over the cliff after their father. Alas, this was not to be and, unfortunately for everyone else, the wolves were allowed to leave the scene of their father's supposed death with their tails very much between their legs. They did indeed learn how to survive. And they did indeed learn quickly.

Despite their lack of experience, they were still from 'good' stock, so to speak, if you could ever refer to the Wolf as good. Perhaps 'evil' stock would be a more appropriate phrase. They had fed well all their lives and only on the best cuts of meat; nutritious and high in protein. The wolves were strong and the fact that they were overweight, gave them an advantage in their struggle for survival. Yes, they became hungry and weak, but their fat stores provided them with just enough energy to make it through the first few days and nights. They scavenged and scrapped for all they could find and it was difficult for them, initially, to get used to the measly morsels of poor quality meats. But they soon became used to smelling out a rotting carcass a mile or two away and gorging hungrily on what was left of it.

As the days turned to weeks and the weeks into months, the wolves found the strength to search further afield for a more suitable dwelling. A quaint little meadow caught their attention and they were particularly intrigued by a rickety old bridge at the bottom of the sloping field. They cautiously eased across the structure one by one, and came to rest on the other side, seemingly safe in the confines of the tall grass. From the top of the ridge within a gap in the treeline, an enormous bellow rang in their ears and they came face to face with Bull for the first time. Although they were frightened of such a large beast, the wolves had learnt that they themselves carried weight in numbers and were able show the bull no fear. Well, very little fear, at least; Bull felt their trepidation as he approached them, but was cautious not to make any sudden movements. After all, there were three of them and he didn't want to ruffle any feathers unnecessarily. To begin with, the bull seemed to take pity on the stranded and desperate wolves and he allowed them to stay, promising himself that he would keep a watchful eye over them. Soon enough, the wolves became comfortable on the island and soon their strength returned; they even posed a threat to the very hierarchy of the islet.

Bull knew that a conversation had to be had with the wolves, to remind them whose island this was and that he was indeed the boss. It was agreed that the wolves could remain on the island, as long as they lived within their means and behaved respectfully regarding natures unwritten rules. More importantly, they agreed not to leave the island. Bull insisted that this was an essential feature of their agreement. It wasn't that he trusted the wolves, far from it, but the threat of his wrath was enough to keep them onside for now. That and the fact that they had everything they wanted on the island and could roam freely, without the fear of being hunted by angry farmers. Since Wolf was no longer around, many of the farmers in the area who still held a vendetta against the evil tyrant went looking for his three offspring instead. Wolf had committed unspeakable, murderous acts against many of the creatures throughout the countryside and as a result, a large number of farms had lost a great deal of business. Another indication that this agreement between the bull and the young wolves was a satisfactory compromise was that the bull fed only on grass and presented no threat to the wolves when it came to hunting for food. There was plenty of choice for the wolves where food was concerned; rabbits, foxes and moles were just a small selection of the many animals that lived in abundance on the island. And despite the fact that the wolves were indeed a formidable team, the last thing they wanted was to get on the wrong side of the huge bull, who could trample them in a flash, should they give him good enough reason.

So that was how things went for the next few months, until of course, Bull and the wolves noticed some interesting activity in the meadow across the bridge. It had been visited by a couple of humans and then some huts and pens were built in the middle of the field. Bull watched with intrigue as the humans then brought into the pasture a brood of hens, a solitary cock and three goats. Bull wasn't only watching the new arrivals; he also realised that the wolves were showing less and less interest in the inhabitants of the island, and more and more interest in the goats and hens across the water. In fact, on one particular evening, just as darkness had settled and the moon's reflection flickered off the ripples in the stream, Bull noticed that the wolves had congregated near the Troll's Arc. He marched down towards them and demanded to know what they were up to. He didn't need to ask; he'd already worked it out, but he wanted them to admit to planning on crossing the bridge. Of course, they pleaded innocence, stating that they were simply out strolling along the river bank, breathing in the night air and appreciating their surroundings. Bull gave them a firm reminder of the agreement they had come to and sent the wolves back up to the trees with a harsh warning ringing in the ears.

"If I ever catch you creeping across that bridge into the meadow," spoke the bull, sternly. "You won't have to worry about where you're going to live anymore; you'll have to worry about staying alive. Leave those animals alone. If they don't bother us, we don't bother them. Understand?"

It was a rhetorical question if ever there was one and the wolves had no interest in providing it with an answer of any kind. There was no sarcastic retort, no witty jib, just a sulking silence as they plodded off back up the slope and disappeared into the treeline once more. Bull was left standing at the foot of the bridge and he looked across at the family of goats, who were grazing in the far corner of the field. He thought it strange that a rooster was sitting with them, seemingly completely at ease with his companions. It almost appeared as though he was one of them, but then somebody must have said something amusing because the three goats all bleated with laughter and the cock let out a cockle-doodle-doo that resonated around the night sky. The rooster was most certainly not one of them, but the ever-intriguing group unquestionably made up a very happy family indeed. That night, Bull made a promise to himself that he would become the watcher of the bridge and protect the creatures in the meadow. He didn't know it at the time, but it was a promise that would be tested a little more than he bargained for.

The helicopter

The morning after Billy's conversation with the bull
arrived and Billy woke up with a start - the whirring of
helicopter blades erupted through the countryside,
destroying the tranquil ambiance and disturbing any of
the animals that were trying to enjoy a few extra
moments of treasured sleep. Soaring above the
landscape, the helicopter roared through the air, heading
right towards the meadow and its adjoining island.
Creatures below looked up angrily at the disruption. A
pair of squirrels rubbed their tired eyes and shook their
little fists at the air. A large eagle, soaring high and on
the lookout for anyone not following the aeronautical
guidelines, had to take evasive action to avoid being
caught up in the vortex created by the blades. With an
experienced twist of the tail, he managed to dodge the air
trap and prevent himself from being sucked down into
the rotors. Looking up at the near miss from his vantage

point of the fence post enclosing Gruff's meadow, a busy robin noticed a large worm trying to bury himself into a particularly soft section of mud. He swooped down and caught the worm just before it disappeared completely. Yanking it out of the ground, the robin flew off with his catch, heading back towards the large oak tree in Hillside Farm, where his nestlings were hungrily waiting their father's return.

Gruff poked his head out of the doorway to his pen and looked up, an irked expression on his face. He followed the helicopter with his stare as it flew above the meadow, low enough to make the taller grasses in the field dance erratically to and fro. The noise eruption continued as the helicopter made its way over Troll's Arc and hovered beyond the treeline, before disappearing out of Gruff's view and coming to rest in the clearing at the centre of the island. The blades slowed and the din quietened down to a subdued hum before they stopped altogether and tranquillity was restored to the countryside. Gruff was joined by his family, all sleepy-eyed and groggy. They stood together upon the hill of the meadow, looking across the stream to the island on the other side.

"What's going on, Dad?" asked Billy, momentarily forgetting all about the bull and the trouble he and Johnny were still in after their escapades onto the island. Before Gruff could reply, Henry the messenger pigeon coasted down out of the sky and came to rest on the roof of the shelter.

"The owner of Buck Lane Grange has arranged for the bull to be carried over to his farm for breeding," informed Henry from his high perch. "He has introduced a number of young cows to his farm and he needs to the bull to mate with each of them, as it's that time of year. Apparently, it has been scheduled that the bull will be anesthetised on the island and carried by helicopter to Buck Lane Grange. He will be returned in a day or two."

Gruff, Sally, Billy and Johnny all stood in a bemused silence in response to this scrap of information. It was possibly a more interesting snippet than any of Gruff's attempts to date. Gruff almost had a look of acceptance on his face that this piece of intelligence was indeed more bizarre and unexpected than anything he'd ever heard before.

"What," he said, almost in protest. "You mean they're going to sedate that huge thing and get him in the helicopter?"

"So I hear," said Henry with a nonchalant shrug. "They certainly won't be able to guide him over that bridge. I doubt that thing is strong enough to allow Billy to walk across it, let alone a huge beast like that." Billy glanced up at Henry, who was looking down on the little goat, knowingly. He seemed to ever so slightly and ever so slowly nod his little head as he looked at Billy. Billy shuffled his feet, uneasily and traipsed down towards the stream; he needed yet more time to take in what he had learnt the night before, and he did not want to come across in any way affected by the pigeon's suggestive remark. Johnny followed his buddy and together, they sat near the stream and looked across to listen to the on-goings from the island.

As the helicopter's blades came to an eventual halt, the doors were slid open and three men dressed in green, jumped out and set off in the direction of the wooded area. They had seen the bull from the skies as they hovered above and were quick to locate him, despite his efforts to find a dark, sheltered area in which to hide. Keeping a safe distance from the bull at all times, as well as a watchful eye for anything unpredicted, the team closed in and surrounded the animal. It was a well-organised operation; they moved swiftly through the trees and tranquilised the bull with an accurate shot in his large hide. The bull gave a jolt as the dart caught him in the rump and after a matter of minutes, he began to stagger, before sinking to his knees and then quietly collapsing onto his side, fast asleep. A large covering was secured around and underneath the huge beast and connected to a pulley in the helicopter. He was then dragged slowly through the forest, while the team of anaesthetists ensured his safe passage; he was a supreme beast. It was a very careful and considerate process and the bull's welfare was obviously their top priority. In what seemed a very short while after the helicopter had landed, its blades were soon whirring loudly again, preparing for take off. Three pairs of eyes watched keenly from the seclusion of some nearby bushes and as the aircraft rose up into the air, they vanished. The pilot of the helicopter squinted down as some movement on the ground caught his eye. Not that he thought anything of it, but he was sure that he saw three shady figures darting in the midst of the trees below. A repeat of the earlier disorder ensued as the helicopter made its way to Buck Lane Grange, although by this time, all the animals had already been woken up. It did however offer them the opportunity to look up and scowl at the noisy machine, and if it took their fancy, to once again shake their fists in objection.

Henry spent a short while at the meadow with Gruff and his family. He always enjoyed laughing and joking with the youngsters, and he had always had a fondness for the couple, ever since he saw how supportive they were of each other during the upheaval of their move to Buck Lane Grange, which felt like donkey's years ago to him now.

"Can Cynthia and Jeremy expect you all at 9pm sharp tonight?" he asked Gruff as they all relaxed in the warm pastures.

Billy and Johnny looked hopefully at their parents, but to no avail. "Well they can expect us," replied Gruff, gesturing to his partner, "but Billy and Johnny will not be attending."

"Oh?" questioned the bird. It was as if Henry somehow already knew the ins and outs of it all, but that he just wanted to hear Gruff's side of things.

Gruff went on to explain why the two of them were not allowed to attend the evening with the pigs. They both looked very sorry for themselves but Henry was in complete agreement with Gruff and Sally's decision, concurring that it was important for young animals to learn that there are consequences for their actions and that rules are set for a good reason. Although they both loved Henry, Billy and Johnny thought that he could be a bit of a fuddy-duddy at times. Perhaps if they knew more about his heroics in the skies, and more about his great ancestry, they would be more respectful and perhaps a bit more wary of the proud carrier pigeon. And just maybe they would realise that he knew more than he was letting on; after all, a carrier pigeon of Henry's esteemed position needs to be in the know of all that happens around the countryside in which he operates.

With the bull gone and the party at Cynthia's fast approaching, it was time for Gruff and Sally to get ready. Henry left with a goodbye coo, along with another telling glance at Billy, who was watching from down the slope. Gruff and Sally disappeared into their pen to prepare and Billy and Johnny remained near the riverbank to ponder how the events of the last few days would impact on their chances of freedom.

Oh Johnny

"So what shall we do tonight?" Billy asked, chewing on some grass.

"Well, there's only one thing for it isn't there?" Johnny replied, excitedly. "We have a chance to go and really explore the island, now that the bull is gone."

Billy almost choked on the grass he was grazing. He couldn't believe what he was hearing. "What? Are you crazy?" he protested, spitting clumps of half chomped grass out of his mouth.

"It's the perfect opportunity," Johnny said. "There are no dangers on that island now, and with Mum and Dad away all evening, we can take our time and find out what it's like over there."

"Johnny, we can't. No way." Billy had been caught completely off guard by Johnny's rebelliousness and had never expected him to suggest another visit to the island, so soon after being caught.

"I know I've messed up a couple of times recently," said Johnny. "But we're not going to get another chance like this. Come on, Billy, it'll be fine. Anyway, I thought you'd be itching to get over there and explore. How come you're so against the idea? Are you a chicken or something?" Billy the goat took immediate offence to this; he was most certainly not a chicken.

"You don't understand!" pleaded Billy. "You think you do, but you don't. We can't go across that bridge and that's final. We're in enough trouble as it is and if we get caught again, there's a chance that Mum and Dad will separate us for good. Is that what you want?"

"Of course not," clucked the rooster, strutting alongside the crooked straight of water that ran between their idyllic meadow and the now ominous island on the other side. "It's just that not so long ago, you were talking about us being able to continue our adventuring, so long as I learn to watch what I say. Well this is my chance to prove that I'm learning, my chance to show you that I won't let you down again." Johnny stopped strutting and looked at Billy, who had been strolling next to the cock as he spoke. He placed a wing between Billy's withers. "We're best mates. We're there for each other, always have been. There are no secrets between us, Billy. None. After everything we've been through, what with dealing with our parents being moved to a different farm, the late night parties at Cynthia's, and now this new place we've come to live; we've stuck together through thick and thin all this time and I'm not about to let a little bridge come in the way of that."

"I know we're best friends, Johnny." Once again, Billy had been caught off guard. Johnny's little speech had struck a nerve and Billy looked down at his trotters, doing his best to avoid eye contact. He shuffled awkwardly in the grass and knew immediately that he would have to tell his best friend that he had indeed been keeping a secret from him. Not just an ordinary secret; a secret of epic proportions that threatened to utterly destroy their friendship. Secrets are essentially lies and, as Gruff had always said, one lie leads to another. Now was the time to come clean if Billy and Johnny's friendship was going to last. "I need to tell you something and I don't want you to get mad," began Billy, hesitantly. "Last night, I went back across the bridge."

"What?" shouted Johnny. "When? How? What do you mean you went back across the bridge?"

"Sssssshhhh!" interrupted Billy, trying to calm the rooster down.

"Don't tell me to shush! How could you have gone across without me?" demanded Johnny.

"Please," begged Billy. "Just listen for a minute." He turned away from the pen at the top of the meadow and beckoned Johnny to join him in an attempted huddle.

"When we managed to get back over last night, after the bull chased us, just before Dad came down, I looked into the bull's eyes and something didn't feel right. Just the way he looked at me, it was weird."

Johnny huffed and started to walk away towards the pen, but Billy grabbed his wing and held him back. They tussled for a moment and things became quite heated. Johnny tried to pull away, yet Billy held on tighter. After more scuffling, Johnny hit Billy on his head with his wing and momentarily stunned the goat. This gave the cock the chance to wrestle free of the goat's grip and he began to saunter angrily up the slope.

"There are wolves on the island!" blurted Billy, as loud as he could without the whole countryside hearing him. Johnny stopped. "The same wolves that Davey, Harvey and Stanley spoke about when they got home after their journey. Three of them."

Johnny turned and walked back to his friend. "What do you mean wolves? There are no wolves over there, your dad said so!"

"Dad doesn't know!" explained Billy. "The bull was trying to protect us. It's true. We talked all about it." Billy looked at Johnny and opened his hooves in a pleading display of regret and sorrow. "I just needed to know why the bull looked at me like that. I knew he was trying to tell me something. I'm sorry I went back over there without telling you. I'll never lie to you again, I promise."

Johnny sat down, seemingly having begun to forgive Billy and evidently becoming more interested in how the information he was being told was unfolding. "You spoke to the bull?"

"Yeah," said Billy, settling down with the rooster on the grass. "He told me that the wolves have lived on the island for a few months. They must have gone there after their dad went missing. He said that the wolves and him had an agreement that they could stay on the island, so long as they behaved themselves."

"How do wolves behave themselves?" spluttered Johnny.

"As long as they don't terrorise the island and only eat what they need to, the bull said that he would let them live there," continued Billy. "He said that it was better to find a compromise with them, rather than let them do whatever they wanted. The bull thought that if they were allowed to cross the bridge, the whole countryside would live in fear, and we would certainly be the first things on their menu. This way, at least they stay over there and kind of live happily, at least without ruining everyone else's lives. They were really angry about what happened to their dad and apparently, they went to the island to gather themselves after losing him. Since then, they seem to have calmed down and settled there permanently, but when we went across last night, all that changed and they nearly caught us. The minute we're on their soil, their territory, it kind of rubs their noses in it and there's no telling how they might react. If the bull hadn't chased us away, we would have definitely been eaten by them. He saved us."

The two of them sat together in silence, with neither of them knowing what else to say. It was clear that Johnny was angry with Billy for what he had done. He felt betrayed and Billy knew it. All of a sudden, Johnny stood up.

"Well, I'm still going over there," he snapped. "How do I know you're not lying to me again? How do I know that there are wolves over there? I haven't seen any and I've spent hours walking up and down this stream. If there were three wolves over there, I would have seen at least one of them by now, surely."

"You can't go over there – it's too dangerous!" said Billy, standing immediately in protest. "You've got to trust me, Johnny!"

"That's just it," said Johnny, sadly. "How can I trust you now after what you did?" And with that, the little rooster marched up to his pen, leaving Billy sat on the grass on his own.

Billy understood that there was nothing he could do, other than watch out for his mate and try to keep him from crossing the Troll's Arc. It was going to be a long night and Billy knew he would have to keep his wits about him. He was determined to save his friend, even if it meant staying up all night. He watched with a glum expression as Johnny entered the pen with disgruntled swish of his wing, without even looking back over his shoulder. Billy had never felt so guilty. He breathed out a sad, long sigh and slumped back down onto the soft blanket of grass. He watched as a little robin fluttered onto one of the posts half way across the Troll's Arc. The bridge gave out a little creak; surely it wasn't going to give way after all these years due to the weight of small robin. No. As sure as night follows day, the bridge held fast, and the robin hopped from one post to the next, chirping happily in the general direction of the miserable goat. Billy blinked back, unmoved by the' robin's energetic little dance. It was going to take more than that to improve his mood.

Just then, a faint shadow crossed over Billy's head, making him look up to the sky. All he could make out was the outline of another winged creature, the sun above blinding him momentarily. Henry expertly swooped into view and perched silently onto the first pillar of the bridge. Despite the fact the Henry was much larger than the robin and surely weighed a great deal more, the bridge made no sound whatsoever as the bird landed.

"I see that you and Johnny have had a little chat," Henry spoke. He obviously hadn't flown off too far and had watched them talk from some hidden position. "By the looks of things, it didn't turn out too well. You didn't tell him that you went back over the bridge without him, did you?"

"Yes," answered Billy. "Hang on, how did *you* know?"

"It's my job to know. How is he?"

"He's not good," Billy explained. "I don't know what I'm going to do."

"Well, so long as you don't let him go over there while the bull is away," Henry warned. It was as if he could read Billy's mind. Billy thought that Henry would have had more important things to do than to trouble himself over two squabbling infants. "I've got more important things to do than to keep an eye on you two whipper-snappers," he said.

"We won't be going back over there in a hurry, don't you worry. We're in enough trouble as it is."

"Good," Henry said, firmly. "I will most likely be out of action this evening as I shall be attending Jeremy and Cynthia's party. I've been looking forward to it for a long time and I don't expect to be disturbed by any sort of shenanigans." Billy felt like he was being reprimanded by an old head teacher. His head sunk lower and came to rest on his hooves. Henry noticed his glum expression for the first time. "Hey, come on now, chin up. There's no use crying over spilt milk. What's done is done. Things could be worse."

"Could they?" asked Billy. "We really wanted to go to the party as well, and now Johnny isn't even speaking to me either."

"Your friendship with Johnny can be fixed," said Henry. "The promise that you broke to your parents cannot. You've got to earn their trust back and that will take time. But they both love you, Billy. You're very lucky to have two parents who are able to put their heart and soul into raising you the right way. Not everyone is that fortunate." And with that, he left the post upon which he had been perched and flew off, high into the air and out of sight over the treeline of the mainland's forest. The little robin popped down from its own leverage point, the bridge creaking slightly as he did so. He grabbed at a large shiny slug at the top of the river bank and, quick as a flash, he was off, back in the direction of Hillside Farm.

All alone, Billy remained on the grass for some time, mused over what Johnny had said, what Henry had said, and what he might do next. He noticed that his parents were chatting excitedly inside their pen, no doubt looking forward to their special evening. Billy was glad for them. They had done so much to look after him and Johnny. He felt that he had taken them for granted and that tonight was their reward for being two of the most fantastic, loving parents a goat and a rooster could ever wish for. He smiled to himself and pushed himself up onto his feet. This was their night and nothing was going to get in the way of that. Not Johnny, not the bridge, not Bull. Not even those dastardly wolves. Billy spent the rest of the evening strolling along the crooked strait, almost in a patrolling manner. He trudged up and down the riverside, sometimes peering at his reflection, sometimes looking around at his picturesque surroundings, and regularly glancing up towards his pen to see if Johnny was going to make an appearance.

Eventually, Sally and Gruff emerged from their pen, both of them smiling and laughing. It made Billy happy to see them like that. He trotted up to them and gave both a hug. The three of them embraced for a moment and Billy told them how sorry he was for letting them down on more than one occasion recently. They explained that they loved him and Johnny very much and that they were only doing their best as parents to make sure their children were safe and learning the right way to do things. Sally explained that although Billy and Johnny were not off the hook, she appreciated his apology and knew that he was being genuine. Gruff put a reassuring hoof over Billy's shoulder and squeezed him tightly. He spoke of how proud he was to have a bright, adventurous and honest kid like Billy. And he told of his love for Johnny. He told Billy to get some rest and that in a few days, all this would be a distant memory. Billy didn't mention anything about him and Johnny falling out. Nor did he tell them that Johnny was thinking of going over the bridge again. That would mean he would have to come clean about the whole thing; the bull, the fact that he went over the bridge a second time, the conversation with the huge beast, and of course, the wolves. This was certainly not the time to get that off his chest. Sally said that they would be home in the morning, depending on how the evening went and whether or not Harvey offered them breakfast. Gruff and Sally departed and threw two or three smiling glances over their shoulders at Billy as they walked towards the gate of the meadow. Billy stood and watched, thinking to himself how lovely his mum looked when she spruced herself up and he noticed just how handsome a goat Gruff actually was. He was strong and powerful, with good posture and a balanced stride. His sharp jawline gave him an almost regal appearance and when Sally walked alongside him like that, Billy thought they looked like a king and queen.

Wolf

On this night of all nights, a lone wolf sat hunched in the darkness of his cave, staring blankly at the wall in front of him. This particular wolf looked hoary and drained. The bones of his scrawny hind legs were crossed on the cold, damp floor and his gaunt face looked miserable and his eyes empty. His matted coat was dull, patchy and grey and his once sharp, powerful claws were blunt, brittle and chipped. One time, this particular wolf was the ruler of the countryside. He used to terrorise the other creatures and the very mention of his name would inject fear and panic into entire communities. He used to be known as Wolf. He was once a strong, powerful, fearsome beast. That was until he took things too far and messed with the wrong family. Three small pigs, to be precise. After Wolf had preyed on their vulnerable mother, Cynthia, they left the safety of their own bedroom and embarked on a treacherous adventure to find their forgotten father and search out the wolf they held responsible for the separation of their parents. The wolf in question was Wolf. The very wolf who lay in the dark, bleak cavern on this very night. The very wolf who had been found by the pigs near the end of their adventure and overpowered by their father, Jeremy; a huge boar who, until the three pigs had found him, had lived in ignorance of the wolf's manipulative interfering with Cynthia's lifestyle. On that fateful night, Wolf had been defeated by the powerful and vengeful pig, and to prevent himself from being killed by one final, crashing blow from the hog's trotters, Wolf had used the last reserves of his energy to throw himself off the cliff edge of Wakeman's Hill and down into the Silkstream River below.

Since that night, Wolf's life had changed forever. At first, he was presumed dead, and every animal in the countryside celebrated joyfully. The creatures could live without fear at last, now that the long line of the Wolf family had been killed off. Opinion was that his pathetic offspring were no match for even a lonely rabbit, who would strike fear into the useless trio with barely a twitch of its nose. For generations, the Wolf family had mauled and murdered their way round the country, killing unnecessarily and mindlessly mutilating creatures for fun. But it was soon discovered that opinion or rumour had been wrong on at least two counts. The Wolf was not dead and his offspring were not the pathetic, useless cretins that they were believed to be. Wolf had somehow survived the duel with the mighty pig. Wolf had somehow survived the tumble down the huge cliff face. Yet more surprising still, Wolf had also somehow survived the long journey down Silkstream River. He had been battered by rocks, pulled beneath the waters by strong undercurrents and dragged along the river bed for long periods of time. However, Wolf had managed to survive; he had bounced off the hard and jagged rocks, he had managed to hold his breath for just enough time when he was underwater, and he had succeeded in gasping life-saving chunks of air, whenever he was above the water line.

Soaked and exhausted, Wolf had pulled himself onto a riverbank and hauled himself out of the water to safety. He had spent a long time hiding in recovery and when he finally had the courage and strength to emerge into the wilderness once again, he was half the Wolf he once was. Literally. He plucked up the courage to visit Hillside Farm, perhaps for one last time, perhaps to confirm that he was indeed beaten by the more powerful animal. Or perhaps to reignite his belief that he was the most fearful beast in the countryside and to set his plan for revenge in motion. Somehow, he made it unnoticed to the outskirts of the farm. Gone were the days of his silky and silent footwork, of his stealthy and sneaky wonderings. Gone were the days of when he was able to creep up on a victim and surprise them. Wolf was clumsy and noisy in his approach; nonetheless, there he had stood, peering through the hedgerows of Hillside Farm. He spent a long hour there, watching, snarling, growling, but nothing more. The very sight of the little pigs playing happily in the mud made his skin crawl.

Then, Jeremy appeared at the top of the path that led down to the pigsty. Wolf had observed in awe as the huge boar stood proudly at the peak of his farm; after all, it was his farm. After the stories of the recent victory over the Wolf, who was going to argue with him? Certainly not the Wolf. He stopped breathing for a moment as the pig surveyed his homestead, powerful and confident, the exact opposite of the figure Wolf had become. There would be no retribution, not today, not ever. Wolf was beaten, defeated, crushed and destroyed. All of a sudden, it seemed as though their eyes met, it seemed as though Jeremy was looking straight at Wolf, almost squinting to look directly at him. Wolf didn't dare move, or even blink. He held his breath for longer than his frail lungs could cope with. To Wolf's relief, Jeremy turned and made his was down to his mud pit. No, there would be no repeat of the epic battle weeks before. Wolf had neither the desire nor the strength to contemplate it; he winced as he recalled some of the devastating blows Jeremy had delivered. Wolf's body still ached and the memory of it all hurt even more. He was no match for the almighty pig and he knew it. He backed away from the hedge and skulked through the woods, in search of a place to stay.

The first creature he had come across, a friendly looking fox, didn't freeze out of fear and then scarper off in the opposite direction. In fact, the fox seemed more intrigued than frightened, approaching the Wolf and sniffing around him inquisitively. The fox seemed to realise who this withered beast before him was and, instead of turning to run, stood tall and proud, face to face with the Wolf. The fox's demeanour changed immediately; his hair stood on end, his claws protracted outwards and his friendly appearance became one of hatred and aggression. Wolf bowed his head in submission and the fox snapped at the frail fiend, yelping loudly at him. Even the very sound of the fox's bark had hurt Wolf's ears and he turned tiredly away and limped off into the forest.

The fox jumped triumphantly and ran, immediately spreading the word about what he seen and what he had done, telling as many other animals as he could find. At first, they didn't believe him, explaining to him that the Wolf was dead or that it must have been one of his useless offspring. But as time went by, and as new sightings emerged, it came to be gospel. The Wolf was not dead. But the Wolf was also no longer the fearsome, terrorising, evil beast that he once was. There was no need to be afraid. The animals of the countryside had something to celebrate again. For some of them, particularly those who had been affected by any one of his many despicable acts, it was almost better that he had survived and he was now a shadow of his old self. The animals revelled in the news and they even sought out the Wolf in the hope that they would find him to verify the story and ridicule him for what he had become.

Much of Wolf's legend was based on the fear that he had instilled in the other creatures. Much of the fear that he instilled in the other creatures was based on his terrible, murderous reputation. The two went hand in hand. But when the animals began to learn that the Wolf was basically harmless, his reputation was shot to pieces and his legend became a laughing stock. Very quickly, the animals became brave, in spite of all the devious deeds he had carried out, and now stories emerged about his frailty and vulnerability. Wherever he went, Wolf was derided and mocked and scorned, even by the smallest and feeblest creatures. Wolf had spent months, desperately searching for some solitude and eventually found it in an abandoned cave atop Springfield Mount. Ironically, it was the same cave that Jeremy had discovered and built for himself a home within years ago. But Wolf had no such desire to make himself a home. The hovel in which he now lay was a world away from the homely, well-furnished abode that Jeremy had created and designed for himself. Wolf was only interested in being alone, away from all possible contact with other animals. Or humans, for that matter.

Wolf had become more than a changed specimen. His instincts reverted and the very nature of his being became backward. Wolf refrained from venturing far from his cave and therefore hunting was out of the question. In the knowledge that animals were unlikely to walk into his dwelling and present themselves to the Wolf for his nutrition, Wolf became dependent upon plants and grasses and weeds. Although his instincts had changed, they were still adequate enough to survive; Wolf even managed to sniff out a particular tomato type plant called Iobeira. He'd noticed it many times before but always turned his nose up at it, most likely due to the belly full of meat he had inside him. Despite the cold weather upon the mountain tops of Springfield Mount, the plant survived and grew well, providing Wolf with much of his now changed diet. With all that he needed to survive – 'food', water and shelter – Wolf had continued to exist in this way until the present day. A lonely, depressing, meaningless existence, but one that many would agree the Wolf thoroughly deserved.

Wolf was particularly depressed on this night. And for good reason. Somehow, he knew it was a year to the day that he had been defeated by the pig. He didn't know how he knew, he just knew. Perhaps it was his instinct again, but he was sure of it. Exactly one year had passed since he had more than met his match on Wakeman's Hill and his life had changed forever. He continued to lie still on the dank, hard floor of the cave. His breathing was shallow and wheezy, as if his lungs were deflated and couldn't hold much air. The cave was silent, apart from the constant trickle of water that ran down the still working spring that Jeremy had devised long ago. As Wolf remembered his heydays; the killing, the feasting, the bullying and torturing, it made him realise all the more just how far removed from his former self he had become. Resignedly, Wolf lifted his head and glanced around the cave once more, as if to say 'Look where I am, look what I've become.' 'What happened to me?' or 'What am I doing here?' There was no one else in the cave to console him or give him any words of encouragement. Wolf didn't have any friends and he didn't know what had become of his children. Not that he had much hope for them; as he recalled, they were hopeless and had no idea how to survive in the wild. But he loved them. They were the only thing in his life that mattered, apart from his reputation and his status of being the most feared beast in the history of the countryside. All that was gone and what was left was a sorry sight indeed. His reputation was in tatters and, what with his current demeanour, he was about as frightening as a daffodil swaying gently in a breeze. Wolf meekly rested his balding head onto his paws once more, as a watery eye blinked and a solitary tear ran down his face, past his dried and thinning lips, and landed on the floor beside his claw. He looked at it and wondered to himself how many more of those he would let out before the night was over.

Here at last

"Sally!" Cynthia cried as she saw her dear friend enter the theatre-like circle that had been prepared for the night's entertainment. "Come and sit down, it's so nice to see you!" Sally sauntered over to the sow, smiling, and the two gave each other a loving hug.

"How are you, Cynthia?" asked Sally. "You're looking so well! It must be all those mud baths! Tell me, how are the boys and how is Jeremy?"

The two became immediately engrossed in conversation and Jeremy and Gruff looked on, amusedly and lovingly. Stanley, Harvey and Davey were rushing around, whizzing in between the goat and their father, handing out flamboyant cocktails, offering freshly prepared canapés and fussing over their guests, checking that everything was running smoothly. They worked together like a well-oiled machine, supporting each other, communicating with darting looks and seeming to read each other's minds whenever anything needed doing. When Harvey needed some limes to spice up his own unique margaritas, Davey was there at his side with a bowlful, already sliced. And when Davey was about to suggest that the entre dishes ought to be collected, Stanley was already gathering them up, on his way to the wash up section, round the back of the service area.

As the party was beginning to warm up, the rest of Hillside Farm was silent. Farmer George and his wife, Mary, were sleeping, blissfully unaware of the goings-on in one corner of their farmstead. Two little robins, having just put their chicks to sleep in their nest, flew from the large oak tree at the back of the farm, and perched proudly in the uppermost branches of one of the trees that overlapped the partying below. As they looked down, they noticed that they were not alone. It seemed as though half the countryside had turned up; the insect half, at least. From ants to earwigs, from spiders to caterpillars, they were all there, sitting or hanging among the branches. There was a hullabaloo like no other, probably not noticeable by the human ear, but from a little robin's perspective, it was like being at the top of a packed out stadium, waiting for the main attraction to begin. The two robins found a comfortable section of the branch and snuggled up to each other, snacking on the occasional grub that happened to cross their path.

Harvey stirred a large steaming pot of dark bubbling liquid with a wooden spoon and dipped in a trotter to taste. A dark burgundy mulled wine dripped off his finger and upon tasting it, he puckered up his chops and kissed his trotters in satisfaction, Italian chef style. The Cleary Sage had indeed done the trick and the wine, which had been fermented from a selection of grapes grown in a nearby vineyard, was, in Harvey's opinion, the best he'd produced so far. Davey perused the menu and, under Harvey's watchful eye, made a few additions to the main course – a delightful concoction of sweet potatoes, mixed together with a variety of other colourful vegetables. It was bubbling nicely in a tomato based sauce and Davey was careful not to overdo it on the salt or the rosemary, remembering Harvey's advice of *a little bit at a thyme.* He would always hold up a small branch of thyme as he said it.

Goblets of the spiced wine were handed out and the guests were treated to culinary delights, the likes of which they had never before experienced. The three young pigs worked tirelessly, waiting on Gruff and Sally, tending to any requests they had throughout the evening, whilst at the same time, ensuring that they too were helping themselves to all of Harvey's majestic meals. As well as the main course, there were other delicious samples to try; in addition to his tried and tested homemade humus and guacamole dips, Harvey had also attempted a cheesy spinach and artichoke accompaniment and he was rather concerned with how it would be received. However, his fears were calmed when he saw the look on Sally's face as took a generous dollop on the end of a crusty bread stick and devoured it hungrily. The cherry tomato and herb puff tarts went down a storm, as did the butternut squash and sage soufflés; a particular favourite with Gruff, who spoke earnestly with Jeremy, all the while inserting the delicate morsels into his mouth. The party was in full swing and everyone was engrossed in each other's conversation, giving the three brothers a moment to reflect and compose themselves before their big moment arrived.

"Lads," Davey whispered to his brothers. "Do you know what the date is today?"

The two of them looked at each other gormlessly, obviously no idea what their younger brother was referring too. He had always been an intelligent soul and was forever informing them of relevant facts, wherever they were or whatever they were doing. And this was no different. In fact, this was quite possibly the most enlightening news that the two pigs would have heard in a long time.

"No, Davey," replied Stanley, juggling some salted and roasted cashews in his trotters and tossing them skilfully into his open jaws. "You know we don't keep tabs on dates and things like that. That's what we've got you for."

"Alright, well I think you two had better sit down, because this is a good one." The three of them huddled together, Harvey and Stanley waiting eagerly for Davey to spill the beans. "Today is the one-year anniversary of the night dad fought the Wolf." It took a moment to sink in. Davey watched as his older brothers digested the information. "It's true!" Davey continued. "One year to the day, exactly. Can you believe it?"

"This calls for a toast!" said Stanley, standing up and raising his tumbler and spilling his nuts on the floor. "To Dad!"

"To Dad!" they all shouted.

The three of them rushed into the circle where their parents and the goats were still talking about fun times at the farm, no doubt reminiscing of when they were all together and life on Hillside Farm was good. The young pigs hustled in noisily, breaking up the ambiance and a hush settled on the group, each member looking at the pigs as they practically fell over each other, stumbling to a halt in the centre of the circle. On-lookers from up above also quietened their chatter and each and every branch of insects and birds fell motionless and soundless. The three of them had to struggle to take it in turns, such was their eagerness to tell their guests, and most of all their father, the auspicious news. In the end, they all spoke over each other but the message was received loud and clear and the party was cranked up a notch or two, with refreshments flowing and yet more tasty mouthfuls being passed around.

It was time for the telling of the tale; the main event of the evening. The young pigs had their moment; enthusiastically describing their brave deeds and courageous acts when searching for their father a year ago. They had told this story many times but never grew bored of repeating it. Stanley spoke in detail of his confrontation with the large, fearsome fox at the base of Wakeman's Hill. He recalled how well the trio worked as a team to disorientate and then pounce on the unsuspecting foxes. Sally winced as Stanley described the sound made when he smashed the fox's head with a large rock. It took a look from Jeremy to remind Stanley to tone it down a little and be considerate of his audience. After all, this retelling of their adventure was not for their own benefit, but for the enjoyment of their guests. It wasn't a horror story; it was a story of triumph and teamwork, of love and fellowship. When Stanley had finished his rendition of the event, he and his audience were both captivated and exhausted, but the pigs were only just getting started and it was Davey's turn to enthral his listeners with his tale of how he saved his brother from the tight grasp of a huge and dangerous snake. Once again, as Davey described the moment when the snake's grip tightened so much around poor Stanley's belly, that he could hear his brother's ribs begin to crack under the pressure, Sally turned into the safety of Gruff's arms. She could be a little squeamish at times and Jeremy put out a large trotter, indicating to the excited storyteller teller to soften the gorier details a little. Gruff smiled and gave Sally an encouraging squeeze; not as tightly as the snake in Davey's story, but tightly enough to make her bleat gently and reassure her that everything was OK.

Harvey for once did not discuss his cooking skills, or explain a new found recipe that he discovered along the way. His part in the adventure was too exciting, even for the talented self-proclaimed chef. Harvey's near death experience on the cliff side of Springfield Mount was an epic rescue tale of strength and desperation. Without his brothers, he would have plummeted to the very bottom and would not be here to relive the account himself. As he spoke, he told of his admiration for his brothers and of his gratitude for their quick thinking and collaboration. There was no wincing from Sally this time, although she did gasp and shudder at the very idea of what the pigs had gone through. The entire audience, the pigs and goats, as well as the crowd above, attended to every one of Harvey's words, so genuinely were they spoken and so earnestly were they delivered. The three pigs embraced at the end of their performance and they were greeted wild whoops and cheers and calls for more from their listeners. At one point, Cynthia was sure that she heard a noise from the trees above and as she looked up, she thought for a moment that the whole ceiling of leaves were twinkling and flustering. It was a beautiful sight and she alerted the attention of the others on the ground. It wasn't that they could make out the individual visitors above them, it was just that when each creature or bird or insect that was in attendance blinked or shuffled slightly, it created a hazy, sprinkling mass of shimmering sparkles. They all gawped in wonder at the sight and it was a while before anyone spoke, as they sat down and relaxed in their surroundings and reflected on the stories and performances they had just been witness to.

And then it was Jeremy's turn. The pigs always loved

listening to their father retell the moment he defeated the evil Wolf. Cynthia always watched proudly as her partner portrayed the scene and proudly explained how he stood up to the then most feared beast in the countryside. Jeremy's story was so full of passion, that it made the hairs on the backs and necks of all those that were listening stand up. It being the one year anniversary of the occasion made it all the more special and there was a triumphant cheer when Jeremy finally got to the part where the Wolf leapt from his cowering position and flung himself off the mountain top to certain death. It was a wonder that George the farmer didn't stir as the cheers and merriments continued after Jeremy stepped down from the slightly raised platform in the centre of the theatre. But nobody cared. If this turned out to be the last party ever thrown by Cynthia and Jeremy and the three pigs, it would have been worth it. If George had come staggering in at that very moment and found them all in their current state, this party would have been the ideal finale to the entire occasion and a fitting end to the celebrations.

Henry, who had been perched at his usual spot, the best seat in the house, smiled proudly as he too remembered his own part in the unfolding of the magnificent story. He flew down and joined in the celebrations, talking with each of the guests in turn and helping himself to the vast selection of remaining appetisers and entrées. He congratulated Jeremy and the other story tellers of their performances and laughed with Sally and Gruff about what a fantastic night it had been. As the hours passed and eyelids began to droop, Jeremy, Cynthia, Gruff and

Sally began to snooze gently in each other's arms. The three pigs ventured over to the bar area, where Harvey began creating some of his unique and stylish cocktails, complete with fruits bits and umbrellas. Henry shook his head slowly in disbelief, not only at the staying power of the three animals but also at preposterousness of it all; three young pigs, having just hosted the party to end all parties and now here they were, tucking into Harvey's Wallbangers. Henry flapped up into the trees and settled for a moment; without doubt, he had an important delivery to make the next day and planned to get some much needed shut-eye. Just as he was dozing off, he noticed something moving in the distance. What it was, he wasn't sure, but it was definitely something heading in the direction Hillside Farm.

At that very moment, Henry also noticed the faint whir of helicopter blades far in the distance. He could not see the flashing lights of the aircraft that would be lighting up the sky if were near, but he was certain that he could hear it. He looked again for the unidentified object that he had seen darting through the countryside below but he could not find it. Had his mind been playing tricks on him or was there something going on that even Henry was unaware of?

When the cats are away, the mice will play, so to speak

Billy had been stressed out all day. Since Johnny had revealed his desire to venture across the Troll's Arc in the absence of Sally and Gruff, Billy had done nothing but worry. He'd worried about his friendship with Johnny; how he had let his best friend down and how his dishonesty and deceitfulness had hurt Johnny so much. The possibility that they would be split up by their parents had also played on Billy's mind all afternoon. Ultimately, it was the danger that Johnny was about to put himself in that weighed on Billy's shoulders the heaviest. Thoughts raced through his mind as he slumped in his pen. If he had just acted differently, things may not be as complicated as they now were. If only he had involved Johnny, or at least spoken to him before stupidly braving the bridge on his own. Billy knew that he had acted with good intentions the whole time; the very reason he didn't tell Johnny about going back to the island was so that he wasn't putting him in any unnecessary danger. But when the thought crossed his mind of how he would have felt if Johnny had gone over there without telling, Billy was resigned to the fact that he was at fault and that Johnny had every right to be upset.

The cock had given Billy the cold shoulder from the very minute he declared his intention to go it alone. Since Johnny had trudged off, leaving Billy to sit and stew on the grass, the two hadn't spoken a word. Billy had tried to make amends, collecting handfuls of Johnny's favourite seeds and sprinkling them delicately in front of him, but to no avail. He'd also tried telling Johnny of some exciting plans to go off exploring in a few days, when everything had calmed down. His efforts were met with a shrug of the shoulders or a roll of the eyes. The remainder of the evening had been spent in silence and Billy had given up all hope of changing Johnny's mind. He had decided to stay awake for the entire night and, if necessary, physically stop Johnny from crossing that bridge.

With their parents away at Hillside Farm, it was all the more difficult to be in each other's presence. They both blamed each other for not being able to attend the party and a heavy, miserable atmosphere hung in the air. It was as though their pen had been enclosed in a cloud of depression and sadness; even opening the door to let some fresh air in only made things worse, because with each gust of air came the slightest noise that could have floated from the farm – sounds of leaves blowing that could have been mistaken for laughter and echoes of vehicles travelling along the roads that made the miserable pair think of all the fun that was being had just a few miles away. Surely it was all in their imagination, but they didn't have to say it; they could both feel it and they both knew what the other was thinking.

As the long seconds ticked by and each minute seemed to loiter like an unwanted smell, it became almost unbearable to remain in the pen. But Billy was adamant that he was going to protect his friend, even if it meant damaging their friendship forever. He couldn't sit still – he used all the tricks in the book to keep himself awake and alert; stretching and leaving the pen for a stroll or a drink of water. He tried to imagine what would happen if he had to actually manhandle Johnny to prevent him from crossing the Silkstream. It would surely have to come to blows; there was no way that the rooster, stubborn as a mule, would simply give in and allow Billy to escort him back to the pen. And how long would it go on for? And how far would it go? Yes, Billy was the bigger and stronger of the two, but Johnny was as fast as lightning and had a vicious streak in him whenever they used to play fight. Billy wouldn't be able to pin him down all night; at some point, Johnny would either need to be restrained somehow, or he would wriggle free and escape across the bridge. As for following Johnny over there, well that was a suicide mission and Billy knew it. Their squabbling would only alert the wolves and the duo would be so distracted by one another's efforts, that they would be unaware of any attempt made by the wolves to capture and subsequently devour them.

It felt as though the minutes had turned to hours and Billy could see that the moon was high in the sky, indicating that it was now passed midnight. He kept glancing over at Johnny, trying to make out whether or not the rooster was sleeping. Each and every time he looked, Johnny seemed to be fast asleep, perhaps dreaming about something amazing. His breathing was steady and the occasional snore made Billy feel all the more at ease; maybe he wouldn't have to restrain his best friend after all. Nonetheless, the young kid was determined to see it through. He rubbed his eyes, arched a spine-clicking stretch and took a few deep breaths to revitalise his energy. Yes, Billy was confident that he would succeed in staying up all night or, in the worst case scenario, stopping Johnny from crossing the bridge. By hook or by crook, he would make it happen; this wasn't the first time that he'd had to keep watch out for one reason or another.

And with that, Billy's head fell heavily upon his shoulder and he was out for the count, sleeping deeply. The poor little goat was shattered and all the drama of the last few days had taken their toll. He had already begun snoring loudly by the time Johnny had crept silently out of the pen. The rooster took one glance over his shoulder as he left, sneering at the goat, as if to say, *I'll show you.*

If Billy's determination was one thing to admire –
managing to keep himself occupied for so long without
falling asleep – Johnny's determination was on another
level. He had remained perfectly still the whole time,
knowing that he was under the watchful eye of his so
called protector. Pretending to be asleep can be the worst
method of staying awake because you have to be still
and silent and you have to breathe deeply. All these
things result in sleep, eventually. And when you take
into account that Johnny had also gone through all the
trials and tribulations of the last few days, just like Billy
had, it was all the more remarkable that Johnny had
managed to stay awake. Rightfully proud of his
achievement, and confident that Billy the goat was
sleeping like a baby, Johnny strutted down to the bridge
with renewed vigour. He shook his tail and ruffled his
feathers in an attempt to prepare and gather himself for
his next task.

Johnny recalled the last time he'd been on the bridge. He
had just escaped the bull's horns and he remembered
how he simply ran across the structure, as if it were
made of steel. *If it held my weight then, it will hold my
weight now*, he thought to himself. He paused. Not in
hesitation, but to take a moment to look around him. He
looked back at the pen from which Billy's snoring could
still be faintly heard; he also glanced at the empty hut
where his parents slept. Suddenly, Johnny felt invincible.
All alone in the dark and no one to tell him what to do;
he puffed out his chest, lifted his head and stepped onto
the bridge confidently. The bridge gave the slightest of
groans as it took his weight, but Johnny just kept on

strutting. He didn't tiptoe cautiously as before and it seemed the more assuredly he placed his claws down, the less of a fuss was made by the bridge. He strode across it and for the first time in his life, he was alone on the island. Alone in the sense that Billy wasn't with him.

But that was the only sense in which Johnny was alone. Of course, he wasn't alone. Far from it. Six beady eyes had watched him stroll down the slope from his pen and pause at the bottom to look around. The very same eyes had watched keenly as Johnny crossed the bridge. At one point, two of the pairs of eyes met, as if to suggest that they were rather impressed with how bravely the rooster had strolled out above the water. But that split second glance was long forgotten and once more, the six yellow and black jewels continued to observe each and every step that Johnny took. Continued to observe each and every breath that Johnny took. Unmoving and unblinking, yet full of desire and intent, the eyes hovered in the treeline, seemingly happy to simply wait for the rooster to come to them.

As a walker would hold a backpack and marvel at the view from atop a mountain he'd just conquered, Johnny stood and surveyed the treeline, his own steely eyes not giving anything away. Yes, inside, he was full of fear, even though he knew that the bull was long gone. But Johnny felt uneasy, as if he was being watched. He put it down to the fact that he was all alone on the island and that his imagination was working overtime. Taking in a long deep breath and blowing it out defiantly at his own emotions, Johnny began to walk up the slope towards the clearing in the trees from where he'd seen the bull appear two nights before. The crest of the ridge approached and the moon, sitting high in the sky, provided Johnny with all the light he needed. He could even make out huge, deep footprints, obviously belonging to the bull. As he stepped over the ridge, the rest of the island came into view and it was a breath-taking sight, even in the darkness. In fact, it was the shine of the moon that gave what was before him an enchanted glow, highlighting the treetops of the forest to his right and glistening magically off the ripples of a large expanse of water down to his left. He could just make out the sea at the far end of the island and he could see a trail that almost flowed through the bushes, right between the lake and forest on either side. He fought back the temptation to skip gaily down the makeshift pathway and monitored the area in more detail before he moved. As he looked at the lake more attentively, he could make out the irregular splashing of what he assumed could only be fish jumping out of the water. It made him feel more at ease that there was indeed life on this island other than that horrible bull. However, the thought did cross his mind momentarily that bears eat fish; Gruff had once explained to him and Billy how, when salmon make their annual pilgrimage upstream, bears feed hungrily on their masses. *But if there were bears on the island, we would have seen them by now,* thought the rooster. And he was right. A glance over to his right revealed a clearing in the middle of the forest, and it made sense to Johnny that this would be the bull's place of sanctuary. When he recalled the helicopter hovering above the island, it seemed round about that location that it went down out of sight and landed.

Happy in his assessment of the island's geographical make up, Johnny thought the best option would be to make his way down the track, between the lake and the forest, to the edge of the island near the sea. He would then relax for a short while, before returning to the bridge, perhaps building up the courage to venture to the clearing on his way back. He began his descent down the slope towards the lake, watching his step as he went. The large, deep footprints left by the bull made helpful, crude steps for Johnny to follow. He could tell that this was the bull's main walkway by the way the path had been worn down. He paused for a moment, and stooped a little as he noticed a different pattern in the earth. Smaller footprints. Lots of them. Johnny crouched down lower to examine the indentations more closely.

And in an instant, they were on him. Strong paws wrapped themselves around his chest and throat. Johnny gave out a terrified squawk before a filthy, muddy claw enveloped his beak and prevented him from crying out any longer. He could hardly breathe as powerful arms and legs enclosed tighter still. Wriggling and writhing with all his might, Johnny was powerless against the sheer force of the wolves' grasps. His wings were pinned firmly to his chest, preventing him from flapping or fussing and even his sharp claws seemed to be hooked together; he was trapped and there was no way out. Battling for air, Johnny slowly felt his strength fading.

His body became limp and he fell unconscious. Only then did the grasp around his entire body loosen. But by that point, Johnny was as out for the count – just as Billy had been the last time he saw him. The devilish wolves dragged Johnny towards the clearing he'd noticed earlier. He had been right about one thing; the clearing was indeed a place of sanctuary. But not for the bull. The clearing belonged to the wolves and it was the only place on the island that the bull did not visit. As part of their so called agreement, the wolves had entreated that in return for their acceptable behaviour on the island, they would be allowed a place of their own that was private to them. Feeling that this was a reasonable request, the bull had agreed to allow the wolves their little space. After all, if it meant that they would be happily confined to one area of the island, the bull was glad in the knowledge that he would have a good idea where the wolves were at all times. But the bull wasn't on the island. There was no one to protect Johnny now and the wolves knew it.

As they reached the clearing, still dragging the dead weight rooster behind them, the wolves strung him up and howled and barked triumphantly. Being unconscious, Johnny was unaware of where he was and, unfortunately for the little rooster, he was also oblivious to the preparations that had been going on, prior to his arrival on the island. The wolves themselves knew exactly what night this was. It was the one year anniversary of their father's demise and they had been busily preparing a banquet in honour of their estranged father. Throughout the day, with the bull gone, the wolves had resorted back to their evil ways and broken all the promises of their agreement. All promises except one. They had not crossed the bridge – that part of the agreement was still very much intact. But they had spent the entire day hunting and killing many of the other animals on the isle. An impressive selection of rabbits, hares, foxes and even moles had been strung up, already expertly skinned and ready for cooking. Although the wolves would usually eat their prey raw, fur and all, on an occasion such as this, an extra special effort had been made. A large pot of bubbling water sat above a roaring fire, flames flashing up the sides as water spat out over the edge. Inside the pot was a selection of herbs, leaves and vegetables that the wolves had scavenged and dug up during the day. Next to the pot was yet another fire, which burned brightly below a sturdy spit roast. Already, an unfortunate rabbit had been stretched out across an iron rod and one of the wolves turned it slowly above the flames, sniffing the aromas in the air.

It would take some time for the wolves to cook and prepare every single one of the animals that they had caught, and Johnny was almost certainly going to be the main event of the feast. The rooster was left dangling from the branches of a tree, while the wolves set about fixing the festivities for their occasion. A rough length of rope had been wrapped around him and he hung there, suspended, the only indication of life was the intermittent inflating of his little chest. Three of the dead animals were lowered into the boiling pot of water and they were prodded and poked until they were completely submerged. The rabbit on the spit roast was removed and placed to one side, and another, already tied to a similar iron rod, was propped gently above the fire and left to cook. It was during this time that the wolves began a ritual-like cleansing of themselves. They washed and bathed each other and combed and straightened their coats. The three of them were sat in a small circle, each one attending to their brother. It was a tender moment that the wolves rarely shared with each other and it was clear to see that they were rather emotional about it all. None of them spoke. Each wolf sat in utter silence, raking the pelage of the wolf in front him.

What will Billy do?

Billy woke from his slumber with a start. It had been the distant howling from across the stream that had stirred him and he looked around his pen, confused and disorientated. It was still dark and the moon could still be seen in the sky through the gaps in the roof. But Johnny was not in his bed. The realisation that Billy had indeed fallen asleep and that Johnny had sneaked out of the pen immediately dawned on the tired goat and he leapt into air with a bleat, crashing through the door, out into the meadow. An eerie silence greeted him as even the water of the stream seemed to be flowing without noise. His head was buzzing with panic and he ran down to the bridge in search of his best friend. Johnny was nowhere to be seen and Billy knew that he had failed in his mission to protect him. He realised that it was now just a matter of time before the rooster was found by the wolves and undoubtedly eaten. Billy crumpled in a defeated heap on the floor and wept. Fond memories of his time with Johnny flashed through his mind. His whole body heaved as he cried uncontrollably into his hooves. There was nothing left to do other than cry. It was too late, surely, to save his friend. All those hours spent frolicking in the meadows, all the adventures that they had been on, all the mischief that they had caused. And all the things they had planned to do together; the secret excursions over the fence to explore inland, the school children at the gate that passed their field like clockwork each and every school day. Life as Billy knew it was over and he found it difficult to contemplate that he might never see Johnny the cock again.

Billy's head rose slowly. He wiped the tears away from his eyes and, with blurry vision, he looked at the Troll's Arc. He snarled and scorned, even growled at the bridge. He wanted to tear it down there and then in a fit of rage. He wanted to smash each slat into a thousand pieces and destroy the bridge until there was nothing left. He pounded over to it and raised a hoof, ready to bring it down on the first slate of wood – the one he stepped onto the first time he crossed it – if only that slate had snapped or broken under his weight. He blamed the bridge for his friend's disappearance and he was focused on one thing and one thing only; to make it so that the bridge never even existed. Eyes wild, tuft of hair on his head twitching, Billy's hoof shook in the air as he gathered up the energy to obliterate that plank into smithereens.

And then he stopped. The thought of Johnny's disappearance, rather than his complete demise, gave Billy an unexpected and renewed sense of hope. What if, just what if, he hadn't ventured across the bridge? Or perhaps Johnny was over there right now, oblivious to the danger he was in, and Billy was about to smash his only chance of getting back to safety. Even worse, what if he had gone exploring and seen the wolves and was right at this moment being chased around the island by the vile antagonists; Johnny was quick but three wolves would surely be able to surround him and catch him with ease. Worse still, what if he had indeed been captured and the wolves were toying and playing with him? Johnny would be terrified and their games wouldn't last long; the wolves would certainly get bored quickly and kill the poor rooster. Billy staggered backwards, his mind continuing to race with terrible ideas of the different situations that Johnny might be in. But in all the scenarios he considered, Johnny was still alive. He gasped, realising that just maybe there was still a chance to save his friend. Whatever choice he made right now would need to be a brave one; almost certainly the most heroic decision he would ever make in his young life.

Billy turned away from the bridge and ran. He sprinted as fast as he could, with no consideration to the possibility that he might have to pace himself. There was no time for getting tired or slowing down. He leapt over the fence of the meadow without giving a moment's thought to the fact that he'd always doubted that he could make that jump. Barbed wire had been wrapped roughly around the top beam of the fence and Billy sailed over it with room to spare, landing in a rolling cloud of dust in the road on the other side. As he rolled, his momentum took him forward and he found himself exiting his roll and bouncing back up onto his feet, seemingly without breaking stride. Billy stormed off into the night, head down, hooves hammering into the earth, flicking up dirt and mud behind him as he went. With no thought for his own safety, Billy continued onwards, darting between trees, leapfrogging large bushes and literally flying across any streams or other obstacles in his way. He tore through brambles that scratched his eyes and ripped at his coat. He stumbled and fell and hit the ground more times than he could remember but, without slowing, got back up and kept on going. The world rushed passed him as he went and he didn't notice the little robin tugging at a resilient worm in the mud in front of him. The robin felt the ground beating and flapped out of the way just in time to see a blur of white flash past him. With the worm still dangling and wriggling in his mouth, he tweeted angrily in the direction of what he believed to be a ghost, before flying off towards his nest in the large oak tree at the back of Hillside Farm. The robin had been in attendance at the party earlier that night, but as the soiree had begun to die down and the storytelling come to an end, he'd sent his partner off to their nest and promised her that he would return with a hefty worm for them to eat before bedtime.

Billy motored headlong into the night. Despite the darkness, he began to notice the familiar surroundings, indicating that he was closing in on Hillside Farm. As he ran, he thought that he could make out the clamour of helicopter rotors in the distance, but he didn't have time to look up in search of the aircraft. Henry, who we know had spotted a strange object running towards the farm, caught sight again of the elusive creature and he worked out exactly what the unidentified object was. It was of course Billy and, alarmed at the rate at which the young goat was travelling, Henry swooped down to inform the pigs below. Billy could see the gates to his old home in the distance. He could make out the top of the grand oak tree that towered over the rest of the farm. The moon sat just behind it, defining the contours of the tree, almost appearing to create the image of a halo around the uppermost branches. He panted and wheezed as he approached the entrance to the farm and darted right, skipping alongside the fencing, in search of the little hole that he always used whenever he and Johnny would sneak out. His head bobbed up and down as he looked for the gap in the fence and when he found it, the gap was filled with a familiar face. Stanley ushered the goat in and the three pigs, Billy and the carrier pigeon all gathered in a worried huddle, just yards away from where Harvey's unfinished second round of cocktails sat at the bar.

"You've got to come," Billy gasped, barely able to get the words out. "It's Johnny. He's on the island!"

"Oh dear," remarked Henry. The three pigs looked at each other, not really understanding what the kid was talking about. "I thought I told you two to stay out of trouble."

"Henry, please!" demanded Billy, desperately.

"Yes, indeed." Henry said, realising the urgency of the situation. "Harvey, Stanley, Davey, get ready, we have to go. Now."

"We're ready," said the pigs.

"Billy," ordered Henry. "You take them to the island and see what you can do to save Johnny. I've got an idea that might help." And without another word, Henry rose into the air, skilfully thrashing through the trees, disturbing hundreds and thousands of sleeping insects as he went. The entire audience that had been witness to one of the most enthralling performances and retelling of a legendary adventure, was until that moment snoozing happily in the shelter of the leaves. Henry's powerful wings beat through the boughs as he took the quickest route to where he needed to go. Many of the insects fell out of the tree, landing silently on the soft grass below. If they had paid in any way for tickets to see the event, they may well have been furious enough to ask for a refund, although so entertained had they been throughout the evening, it was doubtful. The rude awakening that they had all just received only added to the occasion and would merely be another talking point in times to come. Despite the commotion, Jeremy, Cynthia, Gruff and Sally all remained sound asleep, ignorant of everything that was happening around them.

By the time Henry was through the trees, Billy and his

three companions were through the fence, making their way back to the meadow. Although slower than Billy, the three pigs were surprisingly nimble and what they lacked in speed, they made up for in strength and agility. The now seasoned adventurers traversed the fields and hedgerows artfully and were even able to maintain a coherent conversation all the while. Billy explained to them what had happened and even though they were aware of why he and Johnny had been prevented from attending the party, they were still shocked at the fact that Johnny had gone over the bridge on his own, even after Billy had told him about the wolves. When they discovered that Johnny hadn't believed him, it was clear that Johnny was in a world of trouble and that he had gone over there with a point to prove, perhaps not realising the real danger that he was putting himself in.

From the pigs' point of view, it was a chance to rid the world of the wicked wolves once and for all. So confident were they in their prowess over the wolves, the three pigs were almost looking forward to reacquainting themselves with the evil trio. But that soon changed when Billy warned them about how they had, over the recent months, turned themselves into accomplished survivors and more than competent aggressors. As the four of them charged forwards, over the countryside towards the meadow, Billy continued to fill the pigs in on all the background information that the bull had passed on to him. By the time they reached the fence surrounding Billy's field, Harvey, Davey and Stanley were wearing rather different expressions. Gone were the confident scowls and enthusiastic encouragements, and in their place were words of caution and serious glances between each member of the group. Billy prepared himself to leap over the fence once again, still not sure how he'd managed it the first time. As he circled to find the right angle of approach, much like an aircraft awaiting permission to land, he noticed that the three pigs were already waiting on the other side. He looked at them with a bemused stare and it wasn't until Stanley indicated a small breach in the fence that Billy understood; perhaps they weren't magicians after all, like some of the legends had indicated. Maybe they were just very resourceful and observant creatures.

They raced down towards the bridge and sprinted across, with no regard to whether or not it would hold their weight. At one point, as all four of them single filed across the bridge, Billy thought that he felt it move and dip. But they reached the other side without fuss and rushed towards the break in the trees at the top of the hill. Halfway up the slope, their progress was halted by the roar of the helicopter engine. In the time it had taken them to reach the meadow from Hillside Farm, the helicopter had delivered the bull back to the island and was now making its homeward journey back to base. The idea that Bull was back where he belonged filled Billy with yet more hope, even though he guessed that the great beast would still be very drowsy from the effects of the sedatives he had no doubt been given. They watched as the helicopter stormed across the sky above their heads. As they reached the top, it became quite obvious where the wolves were and what they were doing. A warm glow could be seen coming from the clearing that Johnny had observed perhaps an hour ago.

"Look!" shouted Billy, pointing in the direction of the clearing. "Over there!"

Still unseen by Billy and his tribe, the wolves were already eating, tucking ravenously into the first few courses of their meal. Carcases lay strewn about the floor and each wolf was taking it in turn to place another skinned body of meat above the fire. Harvey could already taste the smell of cooking in the air and he thought to himself that he must add a little more basil, the next time he was planning to make a vegetable hot pot. As the wolves continued to revel in their moment, unaware of the encroaching team, they decided together that now was the time to prepare the main course of the evening. By now, Johnny had come round and had spent the last few moments coming to terms with the situation he found himself in. He'd tried wriggling free, but the ropes that were fastened around his body were too tight and expertly secured. He had also attempted to reach one of the ropes with his beak, to gnaw or chew away at it, but it was out of range. And his claws interlocked snuggly together, preventing him from getting any sort of leverage at all. Taking everything into account, it was a desperate situation and he had come to accept his fate. He began to sob quietly to himself, clucking a little and jerking with what little movement he was able to make. And no, this jerking did not loosen the straps around his body either. If anything, it only made them tighter and made it even more difficult to breathe, creating a squeak with each release of air, much like the sound made when a balloon is slowly deflated. So he tried to compose himself. He began to take long, deep breaths, in through his nostrils and out through his beak. Miraculously, it seemed to work. Johnny's breathing slowed and the panic within him subsided. Even the knotted ropes around his body seemed to slacken and it became easier for him to inhale. However, it did not change the fact that there were still three salivating wolves making their way over to where he hung. The rooster, dangling there like a flaccid goose in a butcher's shop, was ready for plucking. He wasn't sure if the wolves would show him mercy and kill him before plucking him, or whether they would be true to form and keep him alive while they pulled each and every feather out of his weakened body.

With both fires still flickering and crackling enthusiastically, the area in which the wolves were conducting their celebrations (if that's what one would call them), was lit up in a warm glow of red and orange hues. The pot of stewing vegetables hissed and steamed and bubbled, and the wolves spent a moment huddled around it like three scheming witches creating an evil spell. The atmosphere in the camp had suddenly become very tense; obviously, the wolves were emotional due to the anniversary that they were observing. Despite having already had their fill of meat and drink, the wolves were eager for more. They weren't intent on eating the rooster out of hunger. It was savage gluttony and greed that now drove their instincts. They prowled over to the terrified bird, revelling in his fear and distress. Even though he was hiding it well, they could smell it off him. The dread oozed out of his very pores. The closer they got, the wider Johnny's eyes became as he watched them advance. As the three of them loomed, they sniffed the air from beneath him. Their true predatory nature was clear to see and, in the same way a frenzy of sharks would stalk and tease their prey, the wolves stalked about on the floor, sliding between one another and rubbing their coats against each other. Johnny looked down, almost mesmerised by the spectacle below him. He closed his eyes and in that moment, he succumbed to his doom. A calmness came over him and he felt at peace. All the events of the past few days and nights flashed through his mind and he felt no guilt about any of his actions whatsoever. He didn't feel bad about treating Billy in the way that he had – they were friends and Johnny understood that sometimes, friends fall out. He thought of Billy and a warm smile grew across his face. Billy was his closest friend; someone he could always count on to do right by him. Johnny felt a sense of forgiveness wash over him. He understood why Billy's actions and the rooster had no grudges or bad feelings about it; he would have done the same.

As far as Johnny was concerned, his slate was clean. The same could not be said for the drooling, greasy jaws that slobbered loudly at his intertwined claws. A large, moist nose sniffed at Johnny's talons and a long, slavering tongue reached out and licked his entire leg. A second nose joined the first and another thick tongue darted upwards. There Johnny hung, beginning to turn and spin as the licking intensified. He felt a slight nip as one of the wolves began to tug impatiently at his feet. The wolves began to snap at each other aggressively; not out of anger, but out of anticipation. They had riled each other up and a sense of urgency overcame them. With a powerful leap, one of the wolves jumped into the air and caught the very branch from which Johnny hung in his teeth. The beast wrestled with the branch, grinding his jaws and flipping his body in an attempt to cut through the wood and bring down what was about to be their final meal of the night. Snapping and tearing at the tree, the wolf used his tail to generate a swinging twist of his body and down he came, branch, leaves, rooster and all. Immediately, they set upon the squawking bird, yanking and gnawing at the rope that entwined his body. Suddenly, Johnny was free; he took in huge gulps of air and for a split second he thought his nightmare was over.

But he was wrong. He wasn't free at all. He lay on his front and he felt the heavy weight of a large paw press him down into the earth. Each of his wings was pulled out and extended along the floor, with yet another hand thrust on top of him to prevent him from flapping. He struggled to breathe once more, turning his head from side to side in a desperate effort to create some kind of airwave. A fourth foot pounded onto his head, crushing it into the dirt. Johnny's eyes squinted under the pressure and it seemed as though his next breath would be his last. Then, Johnny felt a searing pain jolt through his entire body. His worst fears had just become a reality. The wolves were about to show him no mercy at all and the agony he felt rip through him was the pulling of one of his feathers. And it wasn't a quick yank of the feather either; it was a slow, careful pull, and the plume eased out of its well-anchored position, causing Johnny to shriek and writhe and fluster.

Johnny felt another slow tug of a second feather and the pain began to quickly build as the pulling increased. It was worse the second time round because he knew what was coming. Still the pain intensified but still the feather held fast. Johnny began to feel sick. He heard the wolves growling and snarling with enjoyment at the suffering they were causing. And then he heard a different noise. Not a snarl or a screech; more of a squeal. A prolonged, angry, fearless squeal. It was a squeal that shuddered the very ground to which Johnny was being pinned. In an instant, the pain was gone.

Although Henry, the carrier pigeon, was known for his loud call, and was at that moment flying across the clearing, it wasn't he who made the noise. Stanley screamed through the clearing, clambered up onto the table at which the wolves had been dining, leapt into the air and came crashing down onto the group of wolves, sending them scattering in all directions. It was a bold and aggressive move, which set the tone for his fellow attackers. Or were they rescuers? It didn't matter. From a different corner of the clearing, another deafening squeal erupted from the darkness as Harvey pounded into the firelight and charged at the wolf nearest to him, connecting with an almighty crunch. So devastating was the impact, that the wolf was sent somersaulting into the air. He landed in a spluttering and crumpled heap, winded from the blow he had just received and disorientated after somersaulting head over paws. Davey and Billy did not disappoint either, roaring and bleating their way into the fracas and sideswiping an already dazed wolf, just as he was gathering his whereabouts after Stanley's initial onslaught. Davey connected with a powerful clothesline, hammering his forearm into the side of the wolf's jaw, whilst Billy drove his head in low, butting the wolf's behind. He too was sent high into the air; the noise that came from the wolf's lungs sounded more like that made by a frightened sheep. But the wolf's clothing made it very clear that this was no sheep. He landed on his head, bouncing and rolling two, three and four times, before coming to a halt, upsidedown at the base of a tree. His eyes circled as he tried to work out what had happened and where he was. With two of the wolves temporarily out of action, the four crusaders turned their attention the third. So quick were his assailants and so well executed was their attack, he was only now dusting himself down and realising how the tables had been so drastically turned against him. A beating and pounding ensued, the like of which has never been seen before. Frantic blows rained down on the outnumbered wolf and it was Billy who delivered the more telling strikes, wildly butting and ramming with all his might. Battered and bruised, the wolf somehow managed to flee the furore and vanish into the nearby trees. Without a moment's hesitation, the group helped Johnny to his feet and made for the path back to the ridge from which the bull had emerged nights before. In all the commotion, nobody noticed that the sun had begun to rise out of the sea and, as if signalling the way home, shone its rays down on the fleeing creatures, as well as the ridge they ran towards.

Not that they had had the time to wonder where Henry was during all this, but the carrier pigeon was certainly playing his own part in the rescue mission. While Billy and the pigs had been saving Johnny, Henry was busy doing what he did best; making a delivery. It wasn't an assignment that somebody had asked him to complete and he certainly wasn't being paid for his troubles. Nonetheless, it was a mission of utmost importance and one that Henry was more determined to complete than ever before. The pigeon raced to where Bull had been returned to the island by the helicopter. It just so happened that because of the fires in the clearing that could be seen from high above, the pilot of the helicopter had made the decision to drop the bull at the back of the island, near the sandy, rocky area by the sea. It was the only other flat ground that could accommodate a helicopter and there were no trees obstructing its landing or take off. Henry flew down to where the bull lay – he was still sleeping heavily after being tranquilised – and that was where he opened his parcel. A cloud of dust puffed into the air as Henry tore frantically at the paper envelope. He coughed and choked as the smelling salts were released into the air. They settled onto the nose of the bull, who sleepily winced and moaned at the overpowering stench that had travelled up through his nostrils. Henry beat his wings as hard as he could to encourage the salts in the direction of

Bull's enormous face. The bull spluttered and gasped to life, completely oblivious to what was happening. As if waking up into some kind of nightmare, the bull's senses must have been overwhelmed, as he stood and fell and sneezed and spat.

"Quick!" shouted Henry, still furiously beating his wings. "The wolves are about to eat Johnny! You've got to come! This way, this way!" The bull staggered to his feet drowsily and followed the bird. He was still not aware of what was going on, but the urgency with which Henry was squawking and shouting made him trample forwards.

As the escaping group galloped up towards the ridge, Billy looked over his shoulder and saw that the wolves had quickly regrouped and were now making their way out of the trees and onto the path. Even though he was quite a distance ahead, Billy could still make out their ruffled coats and angry expressions. One of the wolves looked particularly enraged and Billy wondered to himself if that was the wolf he had rammed and butted moments before. He bleated to the group to speed up. Meanwhile, Davey noticed something flapping wildly in the air, further down the path. Undoubtedly, Henry was carrying out his part of the rescue, whatever that may have been.

It was an unbelievable scene. Three pigs and a billy goat were escorting a staggering rooster up the path, whilst behind them, three dazed and furious looking wolves were now sprinting after them and closing fast. Further still down the path, a pigeon gesticulated hysterically in the air towards a huge bull, who was beginning to build momentum as he ran.

"Run!" shouted somebody in the leading group.

Panic ensued as they tumbled and fell down the hill towards the Troll's Arc. The meadow on the other side of the river was an uplifting sight, but the wolves emerged at the top of the ridge and flew over it, barking and snapping frenziedly. As they began to descend the slope, a giant bellow thundered in their ears as the bull exploded into view like an erupting volcano. The whole island seemed to shake as the huge beast pounded along the ground, gaining on the wolves with each gallop. He snorted and roared as he continued to speed up. The smelling salts had certainly done the trick; it was almost as if the bull had never been so alive. His eyes glared and rolled as he tried to maintain focus. Was it a look of terror, anger or madness? Who knew? What everyone was certain about was that Bull was wide awake. Perhaps he had been invigorated after his few days away at Buck Lane Grange. As the wolves gave chase, closer and closer they got to the heels of the determined pigs. Billy let out another anguished bleat and Johnny, who by now was fully conscious and flapping and scratching his way down the slope, clucked and clacked uncontrollably. A loud snapping noise could be heard over the ruckus, as the wolves' jaws bit and swiped at their targets. To Billy, the bridge seemed further away than ever before, as he noticed a dark shadow enclose around him and his onrushing friends. At any minute now, he expected to be tripped by one of the evil wolves and torn to pieces by angry teeth. Trotters and hooves and claws became a blur as the little legs that they belonged to whirled faster than the eye could see.

The relentless shadow grew larger and blacker, as the bright sun behind them beamed down over the ridge and was blocked out of the sky by whatever gigantic object it was that was gaining on them. The terrified and panicked group was now in darkness, yet each one of them resisted the urge to turn around, knowing that it would slow them down just enough to be caught. Still the ground shook as Bull blasted down the hill. His momentum continued to build and his speed continued to increase. Harvey was sure that he felt the breath of one of the wolves on his hind legs. He gritted his teeth even more, the muscles in his face tensing and the ones in his legs screaming. Faster they ran, louder they screamed, and still the bridge seemed unreachable.

Davey wasn't sure what or who he was running away from. Was it the furious and ferocious wolves, who were hell bent on capturing those responsible, not only for ruining their important evening but also for destroying their father's reputation? Or was it the huge beast that now boomed and bellowed its way down the slope towards them? He couldn't work out which fate would be worse; to be eaten alive by the wolves or trampled to death by the bull. But he certainly wasn't going to wait around to find out. He motored onwards and downwards, beginning to feel dizzy and nauseous. Stanley, always the more lithe and powerful of the three pigs, was in front of his brothers and beginning to realise that this was a save yourself situation. It wouldn't have made sense for him to slow down to assist; he would only have got in their way, hindered their progress and would probably have been responsible for them all being caught. Like the others, Stanley's heart was racing; his eyes bulged and his little lungs gasped for air, as he became more and more convinced that somehow, this already dire situation was at any moment, about to take a turn for the worse.

Harvey, understandably the slower of the three pigs thanks to his love for cooking (he was always double and triple checking his cooking as he went, meaning that he had usually eaten a full meal by the time dinner was ready), raced along behind his brothers and, aside from Billy, was the one in the most perilous position. He could smell the wretched wolves close in on his behind and he pictured himself laid out on a banqueting table, apple in his mouth, well-seasoned and accompanied by all the necessary trimmings. He visualised the wolves positioned around the table, hungrily waiting for their portion of pork; napkins tied around their necks, knives and forks held at the ready. His mind almost wondered off completely and he had to shake himself back to consciousness and concentrate on his own survival. Adrenaline pumped through his little legs; if he hadn't had the head start on the wolves that he did, he would have been brought down and surrounded long before he even got to the top of the ridge. Lactic acid screamed in his muscles and the pain was becoming unbearable.

Another mind splitting roar from the bull was all the incentive Harvey needed to not slow up. He looked ahead and saw that the bridge was at last a little closer; but it didn't take a genius to work out that they weren't all going to be able to cross it at the same time. Certainly not three or four abreast; the bridge was too narrow. They would need to sort themselves out into an almost single-file formation by the time they reached the bridge.

Not one of them had considered the possibility of the bridge collapsing; their minds had been somewhat preoccupied with their rescue mission. For all its years and for all the tales associated with it, one would have thought that the idea would have crossed their minds. *What if the bridge collapses as we cross it?* The only experience the pigs had of swimming was playing in the mud pool; their doggy paddle was not strong enough to keep them afloat in the calmest of waters. Billy and Johnny had never been in the water and they weren't interested in learning to swim right now. As for the wolves, ever since they witnessed their father tumble off the side of Wakeman's Hill, they had developed a natural fear of the water; the trauma of seeing their heroic dad leap off the cliff and cartwheel into the raging river below had given them nightmares that had taken many months to get over. They weren't prepared to enter the water, not even for a tasty meal combination of pork, chicken and lamb. And then there was Bull. He was a competent swimmer, in deep water. But the Silkstream River was of a depth that meant the bull would have to walk across. The riverbed was soggy and soft and the bull knew that he risked being stranded in the sticky sludge if he attempted to wade across. He didn't much fancy the idea of getting stuck in the mud; that was a game he was happy to watch others playing in the fields and he certainly didn't like the idea of drowning in the stream.

The Troll's Arc

In a crescendo of bellows and barking and screeching and squealing, everything seemed to happen in an instant. The bull trampled one wolf, making him yelp and stumble. At the speed he was travelling, the wolf had no option but to tumble and flip, over and over. Bull rushed onwards and body checked the second wolf, sending him flying into the long grass, disappearing into a cloud of dust and throwing mud and debris into the air as he went. The bridge appeared at last, as if out of nowhere. The final wolf managed to grab hold of Billy's trailing leg, but couldn't get a good enough grip to hold on to it. The goat faltered and cried out in despair, but Bull was already on top of the wolf, charging it with his huge horns and tossing it into the air. The wolf yelped in pain as the bull's horns caught his coat and ripped his tough skin. He was flung like a ragdoll and bounced, lifeless on the ground.

Johnny was the first to hit the bridge, at an alarming speed. Surely, the clamour and fuss with which he was attempting to cross it would bring it down. But he flapped and squawked his way across, without as much as a whimper coming from the ancient structure. Stanley, Davey and Harvey were right behind him, bounding onto the bridge rowdily one after the other. The boards creaked; the poles swayed and the bridge seemed to expand somehow. They were half way across and as Harvey pounded onwards, a slat came loose and snapped, falling into the waters below. Harvey was lucky that his trotter didn't fall into the gap; if his leg had been wedged in the hole he'd just created, he would have either broken it or been trapped. And that only meant one thing; certainly the wolves would have caught him then. The bridge groaned and swelled under the weight as the three shattered pigs pulverised the wooden boards. Surely this was the first time in decades, nay, centuries that the bridge had had to contend with such a load. Billy, having faltered after being nipped by the gnashing jaws of a desperate wolf, was the last of the leading pack to reach the bridge. As he sprinted onto the wooden boards, bleating and crying, he stumbled once more, this time out of sheer panic and exhaustion. Johnny and the pigs were just making it over into the presumed safety of the meadow and Billy's blunder sent him rolling across the rickety structure, bouncing and bashing his way as he went. Every single slat seemed to wince and, just as Billy was edging towards safety, he clattered into the last post and it splintered on impact.

The post gave way and shards of wood were sent flying in all directions. The Troll's Arc slumped sideways as one of its main supporting legs fragmented and split.

Henry observed from above, helpless. There was no way he could intervene at any point since reviving the bull. Yes, he'd been able to coax the sleepy beast up the hill and squawk encouragement and instructions from above, but from the moment the bull had started running, Henry's job was over. That hadn't stopped him from getting a good look at the events taking place below him. As the chase ensued, he swooped down to try and distract the wolves but they were too enraged to allow their attention to be diverted away from the three pigs in front of them. Henry was the only one who'd had the foresight to consider the implications of everyone running across the bridge at once. Despite the chaos below, he'd looked ahead and wondered to himself, *how on earth are they all going to get across without it collapsing?* But that was all he could do about it. He couldn't warn them or fetch help and he had no more packages to deliver that would have been have been of any use. Henry flew higher and hovered. And he understood what the bull was about to do. He almost stopped flapping his wings as the realisation of what was about to unfold dawned on him.

For Bull, this was a different proposition altogether. If he had had a choice, he would have slowed to a standstill and stared triumphantly across at the animals he had just saved. But Bull had gathered so much momentum and the bridge had come up on him so quickly, there was only one thing left to do. Just as Billy was half way across the bridge, tumbling and bumping into seemingly every post and plank, the bull's mind was already made up. Billy landed in the soft grass and ended up with a huge tuft of it in his mouth as he came to a stop, while Bull powered onto the bridge and immediately felt it give way beneath him. Slats warped and exploded, posts that had stood the test of time, bent and buckled. With the bridge already collapsing into the water, Bull bellowed again. Was it a cry of fear, despair or determination? Whatever it was, it was a bellow that would undoubtedly have woken Jeremy, Cynthia, Sally and Gruff from their slumbers, just a few miles away. Stanley, Davey, Harvey, Billy and Johnny were mere onlookers. The gigantic bull's final leap from the failing boards was a sight to behold. Everything went silent and seemed to happen in slow motion. The audience stood with wide eyes and open mouths. Even a little robin, who moments before was tugging at a sizeable worm, dropped his catch onto the meadow's soil and watched in awe as the bull literally flew through the air.

If the ground had shaken when the bull was chasing the wolves down the slope, it was nothing in comparison to the thunderous crash and rumble that was made as he landed on the other side of the Silkstream River. Huge tufts of grass were flung into the air and, almost like the tire tracks left behind by a landing plane, the bull created two or three huge lines of mud in the grass as he skidded and slid his way to cumbersome halt, perhaps thirty feet away from where he had landed.

As for the Troll's Arc, there was nothing left. Not even a post to signify that a bridge had once stood there. No indication whatsoever that the historic structure had ever even existed. All the memories of travellers, all the stories and all the legends were gone in an instant; along with any threat that the wolves would be leaving the island anytime soon.

Bewildered and infuriated at having lost his prized catch, the robin huffed and flapped away, in search for something to take back to his nest. He stopped in a tree on the outskirts of the meadow, landing on a branch and looking down at the scene below. He fluttered his feathers and shook his head, as if to suggest that he didn't quite believe what he had just witnessed. As he looked again, he almost expected the meadow to be empty and he would be able to put the last few moments down to a simple daydream. Alas, no. The animals were still there, all of them; the pigs, the goat, the cock and of course, picking his huge frame up off the ripped and torn grass, the bull. The robin glanced across the Silkstream River at where the Troll's Arc used to stand; his favourite vantage point – the creaking post from which he used to watch for worms poking their little heads out of the soil – was gone forever. There was nothing left of it. Further downstream, the robin could just make out what looked like slats and planks of splintered wood, drifting on the surface of the strait; the final remnants of an ancient structure, destroyed in a matter of seconds. The robin noticed a wolf stirring in the grass on the island. It was limping badly and nursing, among other injuries, a nasty gash on its hind leg. He saw the three wolves huddle together, their demeanours downtrodden and defeated. The robin decided that he had had enough excitement for one day – after all, he'd nearly been flattened by a flying bull. He turned and swished through the leaves to pick up a tasty grub of some kind on his way home; he had mouths to feed.

Each and every creature had its own reasons to be slumped in an exhausted heap on the ground and breathing heavily. Billy lay on his side, taking in huge gulps of air. He had spent the previous day stressed out about his friend, Johnny. He'd been planning a million different ways to prevent the rooster from venturing onto the island and had done his best to stay up all night, in the hope to save Johnny from certain death. Billy had failed in his attempts to stay awake – he hadn't realised just how tired he was and he'd fallen asleep within ten minutes of settling down with the intention of staying up all night.

Johnny the rooster was flat out on his back, his wings spread-eagled and his claws sticking up, pointing to the sky. He had indeed stayed up all night, waiting to be sure that Billy had fallen asleep. From that moment, the poor rooster had been to hell and back; ravaged by three wolves, tied up and dangled in a tree awaiting his turn above the fire. Johnny had been ambushed and kidnapped, licked and bitten, teased and plucked. He had even accepted the notion that he was going to be eaten and had simply asked the universe for it all to be over quickly and painlessly. His answer had been blunt and truthful – the slow and painful pulling of his feathers had been an indication that there would be no swift death. Johnny blinked in the sun as the events of the last few hours began to take shape in his mind and he began to cry, not for the first time. But this time, Johnny was crying tears of relief and liberation, not of fear and hurt.

The three pigs were looking at each other as they lay still, catching their breath as well as their whereabouts. They had also been up all night, but for completely different reasons. It had been a party to remember ay Hillside Farm and they were sure that it would still be in full swing if they hadn't been interrupted by Billy the goat. So taking into account the fact that they had been working hard all the previous day to organise their party and make sure everything was in place, and they had been partying all night, eating and drinking the finest foods and cocktails, it was no wonder that the three of them were now slouched on the grass, recovering.

Bull was somehow on his feet. Understandably, he was unsteady on them, but nonetheless, he was still standing. Perhaps the remains of the smelling salts were keeping him going. The bull had been tranquilised days before and airlifted to a location where he had spent more than twelve hours of sunlight mating with the cows of an entire farm. He'd then been sedated again and returned by air to the island, before being woken up after a matter of minutes by a frantic pigeon flapping smelling salts in his direction. Of all the animals involved, maybe it was the bull who had the right to claim the unwanted trophy of being the most exhausted. Don't forget, he'd also destroyed an ancient, legendary bridge, whilst at the same time, becoming the first ever bull to actually take flight.

On the other side of the crooked strait, the wolves were licking their wounds and making their way back to the sanctuary of their sheltered clearing. Now that there was no way for the bull to make it back over to the island, the wolves had the isle to themselves. Not that they had realised this yet. They were sore and demoralised, miserable and beaten. For the second time in a year (exactly a year), the long line of the wolf family had taken a huge blow to its reputation. Once again, members of the detested and once feared family of evil had been outfought and outthought. And once again, those dastardly pigs had been involved. However, they couldn't be held directly responsible this time. No, this time, it was a billy goat who had masterminded the whole thing. And it wouldn't have been possible without the help of a plucky rooster. Three wolves, powerful, fearless and ferocious, had been defeated by a cock and a goat. Yes, their reputation was indeed in ruins. In fact, their life on the island would almost certainly be very different from now on, without the bull to protect them from the rabbits and foxes and moles, all hell bent on exacting their own revenge on the pitiful so-called wolves. Billy watched them as they shambled up the slope towards the ridge, and they were a pathetic sight to behold. For a moment, he almost felt sorry for them. For a moment, he wondered if perhaps they would learn from this lesson and become better creatures as a result.

Just for a moment. And then he smiled; a victorious and gleaming smile. It was a grin that cannot be faked or rehearsed. It oozed pride and completion, fulfilment and excitement. He looked over at Johnny and realised that he too was wearing the very same expression. The two of them embraced and laughed and hugged and danced, before falling over again through sheer fatigue.

Oh how the animals of the countryside would love to hear about this one – a tale of courage and daring nerve, a story of betrayal, forgiveness and loyalty. The pigs were probably already planning their next night of entertainment; it was only hours ago that they were thinking that their own adventure would never be topped. Imagine what Jeremy would say when he heard of these deeds of bravery and downright heroism.

Imagine

And imagine what Gruff and Sally were going to say when they returned… And just then, Billy and Johnny looked at each other once more. Their grins were gone.

"What on earth is going on here!" shouted Gruff.

"Oh my!" exclaimed Sally, as she noticed the mudslides made by the bull's crash landing. "Look at my meadow!"

Gruff looked at the bull. Sally looked at the three pigs. They glanced at each other and saw Henry swoop down to join them on the grass.

"You have got some explaining to do!" said Gruff, glaring at Billy and Johnny.

And he was right, they did. They had escaped with their lives, but by the look on their parents' faces, the hard part was yet to come.

As you have now read my second book, I once again request your thoughts. How was it for you? I have loved writing this book – like the first one, it's connected me to lots of people and brought me hours of enjoyment and amusement. I hope you have had fun reading it, as that was my main goal – to spread a little joy and laughter about the place.

Thanks to all those who helped in the writing and proof reading of The Crooked Strait; I have appreciated all the feedback I've been given.

Printed in Poland
by Amazon Fulfillment
Poland Sp. z o.o., Wrocław